LOVELESS

Book 1 of the Resonance Trilogy

Chris Luchies

I would like to thank Sarah McQuade (soon to be Luchies) for believing in me and telling me to go forward with the publishing of this book.

I would also like to thank Teghan Ives for helping me with the original ideas and giving me the courage to continue with writing and with showing me the means to publish.

Finally, and most importantly, I would like to thank God for giving me the ideas for this and giving me the drive and ability to finish it.

Contents

Chapter One- Of Death, Destinies, and Doubt 1

Chapter Two- Of Dreams and Decisions 11

Chapter Three- Of Days Gone by and Discoveries 26

Chapter Four- Of Defining Times and Deepening Relations 38

Chapter Five- Of Delusions and Dalliances. 47

Chapter Six- Of Disreputable Events and Drawing Closer 63

Chapter Seven- Of Danger and Disaster 76

Chapter Eight- Of Departing and Driving 91

Chapter Nine- Of Deception and Daedal Diatribes 103

Chapter Ten- Of Demons and Diminishing Dominance 121

Chapter Eleven- Of Deepening Relationships 138

Chapter Twelve- Of Diving in and Divine Beauty 149

Chapter Thirteen- Of Debacle and Debate 158

Chapter Fourteen- Of Dates and Devotion 158

Chapter Fifteen- Of Defining and Deciding 191

Of Epilogues and Emanations 202

Chapter One- of Death, Destinies, and Doubt

There was an article, a while ago, which was written in the Oxford Times about the problems involved with divorce. Throughout the article, they posited facts about the hatred that develops after a relationship split. To drive home the point, they used an example of a couple who broke up because of petty squabbles and little fights. Throughout the trials and processing of their divorce, a distance grew inside of each of their hearts. However, the man had a longing in his heart. He wanted to have her back but didn't know how to approach it. So he started following her. Every night watching outside her window, every day following her schedule. After a couple months of stalking her, he wanted more. He missed her touch, her love, her compassion and the time they spent together. His plan was to approach her while she was home and to apologize for falling out of love. After a few more weeks of planning, he purchased some flowers and wrote a note for her. Then he went up to her door, hoping to reconcile.

The only problem with his plan was that his stalking had not gone unnoticed. She rapidly grew wearisome and afraid. Taking to locking her doors and windows every night and even purchasing a gun just in case anything happened. The more time that passed the more she expected him to harm her. So when he knocked on her door, she searched for the gun and couldn't find it. Seeking for something to protect her, she went into the kitchen and searched for a knife. Her mindset was so skewed because of the hatred in her heart and the stigma of divorced couples that she thought he was at her door for malicious reasons. That is why, the moment she opened her door, she stabbed him.

A few hours after the tussle a neighbor came to check on the lady. She had set it up that once a day her neighbor would come to make sure that she was fine. When her friend knocked, and no one answered, she decided it would be better to go inside. She found both of them lying dead in the middle of the floor in the front hallway. The letter and flowers were scattered off to the side of the bodies. Of course, the cops were called and they looked into the situation. It turns out that they died purely because love had been confused. He loved her, always had and always would. She hated him, didn't trust him and had fallen out of love with him.

Every time I tell that story I get sad. It shows a digression in the way people show affection to each other. Love was slowly decaying in a world that so heavily needs love. The Creator meant it to be the most important thing in our world. Above everything else is love, followed by hope and faith. That is why I exist, to work to keep some sentiment of love. My name is Cornelius Strange. I am a creature of myth that runs in one of three main societies that make up The Three. The Three are the Loveless, of which I am a member, the Hopeless, and the Faithless. Each a corporation whose sole purpose is to follow the Creator's demands and to keep their specific namesake alive.

My job was to make sure that I kept love alive. The basic idea of my Job was to keep one man from making bad decisions in love. All the while slowly leading him towards his soul mate, no matter the stigmatisms he has for her. The rules of my job are simple. Stay in the shadows, succeed at all costs, and never, in any way, fall in love with a human. These three rules are simple and they have governed our society to the point that no one had discovered us yet. We are your conscious, your nagging intellect, that man on the street that brings up love for no apparent reason. We are all around you and yet never truly seen.

We hide well because we look like the rest of humanity though we are not human. Our genetic makeup is completely different. We are called the Resonance by the Master. Probably because of our inherent nature to be the echo of his attributes. We look relatively human though we have the ability to change our look whenever we please. We also have wings that protrude from our skin when the situation calls for us to fly. Though to look at us at face value, you would think we are human. There have been times where we have been confused for angels with our wings and our natural beauty, but we are not His high ups. We are just another creation meant to serve alongside the angels.

My story is a simple one that starts the day after that poor neighbor tripped upon that wretched scene. The man I was assigned to was named Steve De'Lemit. It seemed to me that he was Irish with a bit of French in his background. It was relatively difficult to meet your clientele and still hide in the shadows. Although there were a select few, a sub-sect of our society that does. They befriend their clientele, give them hints into their relationship, and be there for them every step of the way. That takes energy, dedication, and planning, so most of us disregard that as a true method. This, however, does break the first rule of the society. Breaking the shadows rule would be cause enough for you to be suspended from the society.

Should you fail in your mission and break the second rule about succeeding at all cost you would be branded as a failure and more often than not wouldn't be called on again by the higher ups. Finally, there were the ones who have fallen in love. To do this would be the equivalent of asking for humanity. As a Resonance, we are to be above the humans and not of them. To show love, but never to accept. If they break this rule, they pay a hefty price. They go through a painful process to remove their wings and they lose all of their inhuman abilities. These include powers such as healing, immortality, shape-shifting, and a few others that we used to protect ourselves. They are then tasked with making the one they gave up their powers for love them. More times than not it doesn't work.

This is my story, from the beginning as an account for my actions. My reasons and my understandings. As I said before, it starts with the couple who died. Tom, the man who died during that tragic incident, was Steve's brother. I learned this while he was at a diner awaiting his food order. He had just received a phone call regarding his brother's death. I seemed to recall hearing him swear over and over again. For some reason, he thought that this vulgar language would help get rid of his feelings of contempt for his brother's wife. She was a vile lady whom he had never liked. Over the years, Steve had come to dislike her more and more because of the way she treated Tom. Always bickering over unnecessary topics. At one meal with her, she started an argument over the way potatoes were supposed to be made, of all things. At the end of that meal Steve had asked that she not come the next time, they would meet.

Considering all that, Steve still had some sympathy for her death. Every third word I could understand had to do with her. As a whole, it was all incoherent babbling "I... him... Sarah... what... wow... Sarah... I can't believe... Tom... Tom...." His voice trailed away as the tears began to flow. Utter sadness overcoming him as the realization that his brother was dead hit him.

Tom and Sarah De'Lemit died on august 4th 2011 a murder-suicide caused because of a fallout in love. The formal report described the scene in its entirety. How Tom stalked Sarah for three to five months before that fateful day. Sarah's growing paranoia and distrust of her ex-husband. The purchase of the gun from a less than reputable establishment. The tussle at the front door and the note. The note that changed everything about the situation. The note seemed so insignificant at first, but reading through it opened my eyes to a love hidden deep within Tom. The letter stated,

"Dear Sarah,

I am so sorry that you were wrong about us. We could have worked out our differences, we could have been happy. We thought we would be together forever. But we were wrong. There is something drawing me back. A longing in my heart, a feeling I can't control any longer. Something I haven't felt since that first encounter so many years ago. That is why you saw me more these past few months. However, I didn't know how to approach you so I just followed you. The words would never come and the fear of what you might say got to me. I know it wasn't right, I know I should have just approached you, but I thought maybe you would be charmed by my dedication. I wanted you to know I was still there, even if it was only from a distance. I guess all that's left to say is I am so sorry and I love you.

Love,

Tom"

The letter was read hundreds of times during the process of trying to determine the cause of death. They thought of how they could twist the message so that it was him that caused the death. Turn it into some form of evidence against him. Though no matter how you read the letter the message was quite clear: "I am sorry." The whole aspect of the letter confused me. He had lost his chance for love and that was when "love" affected him most. Why was it that humans always loved once their chance was gone?

Tom had been cremated while Sarah's family insisted on a burial; however, the one thing that shocked most people was the group funeral. They shared the funeral home to reduce costs. In the end, it was their death that kept them together, so it seemed. This was the first time I saw her at the funeral, her green eyes glowing in the dim atmosphere of the sanctuary. She had medium length brown hair that always seemed to glisten as if by magic. She didn't just walk, she swayed into the building. Knowing that she was beautiful. And she was, she was the essence of beauty.

Her name was Roxanne Gersch, to meet her it would be near impossible to tell her background, seeing as her bright complexion, light freckles, small nose, and thin body were condoning of a Swedish background. However, she was Russian with a bit of German. She was the girl Steve was meant to be with. My female mark. She was the perfect girl. Every time she would walk into a room, I would look because time would seem to slow, everything stopping as if to admire the angelic figure that came in. Saying all this, she was human, so she was off-limits.

I shifted just a slight bit thinking that they might know where I was in the room. Being so close to them both together was uncomfortable. It was not the norm for me to be in such close contact with my marks. I have walked out on the street before to give a passing comment to either of them, but to stand static in a room with people all around me passing by was nerve wracking.

The room was medium sized with a greeting area to the front and a large milling area at the back. There were doors and offshoots to different rooms, one of which being the sanctuary where the funeral service was held. An artist's rendering of the Master's son was hanging on one wall in clear view of everyone. I stood near the back of the room right beside a large bouquet of flowers that hid most of my body. Even with that, no one would recognize me because none of them had met me before. I was wearing a dark blue pinstripe suit with a light blue button-up shirt underneath. A large brimmed hat topped off the fanciful attire in order to shade my face from onlookers so I didn't have to shapeshift to match the look of the rest of the humans.

One thing I feel I should mention at this point is how love in the Resonance society worked. All the female Loveless were open for business, so to say, and waiting for any guy to pick them up and use them in any fashion. The men would use and abuse the ladies taking them for the prostitutes that they were and never settling down. Having children in the society was odd and rarely happened. Though, for me, I preferred the juvenile approach to love that the humans would take. The chase, the fight to show love, going through the awkward stages of learning about your partner. All of it seemed so much better than the easy to attain women of the Loveless society. Most of the guys would rather be lazy and if they actually did their job they would just go back and find another Loveless woman to blow off some steam with.

Love consists of two steps for the Resonance. The first is an initial statement of love. A pick-up line for lack of a better term. After that, they would flee away to a secluded place and lay together. If a child was conceived they would stay together to tend to the growing but after the child was born it was on to the next person. The baby left to fend for itself. Often, not surviving for long. Sadly, this was where the humans were at in the current society. Prostitutes were ruining what was left of that once amazing emotion called love. Prostitution was the number one industry of two hundred of the two hundred and four countries. Because of that, the society of the Loveless was becoming more and more unnecessary.

Love was going extinct because we started to just not worry. After our society lost the impression of love there was not much else we could do, so we all started messing with the humans. Meddling in their relationships and trying to ruin the experience for them. After that, humans were confused about love and started to marry for the wrong reasons. We caused this falling out in love, but we couldn't do anything about it. We were getting more powerless and it was all our fault.

After looking for a while after the funeral, I finally noticed Steve walking around talking to his family members. Steve was a fairly average man. Average height, average hair, average blue eyes. He was average no more, no less. Which is what confused me most about this mission: Why would someone so utterly beautiful fall for someone who was just average? Steve did have something going for him. He had me, and I was the only Loveless that still cared about his job. These humans, no matter how degraded and dysfunctional their dealings, held a certain place in my heart. A place I just couldn't get rid of, no matter how hard I tried. It seemed like the Angelic head of the Loveless facetiously told me that this could be the last assignment, for anyone, ever. My natural inclination then, was to try as hard as I could to correct their view of love.

Love was becoming a nonsensical idea. The idea of love in its essence has been so flawed people have started to confuse themselves with the idea of it. They started using love on items, on animals, and even on people of the same sex. It has been just a term, no longer a verb, but just an adjective used to express a fondness for an item. "I love that cheese" was not something that was uncommon. But love is so much more. It doesn't fail, or fall, or flee, or refrain from fighting. It is a powerhouse of an emotion that levels city blocks and forces sane people to do insane things. Now, I'm not saying that people cannot be confused about love from time to time, you would have to be beyond human to fully understand it, but to go as far as saying you love a toy or love your car is just insane. True love, that feeling that cannot be controlled, I just couldn't see anymore.

Steve was my one chance to open up that connection to true love again. He just had to fall in love with that one girl who he had always loved. I had been watching him for over two months waiting for a chance to push him in the right direction towards Roxanne, but every time there was a chance he would run away. It was that innate fear that came from the confusion of love.

The fear of rejection. In his case, there was something wrong with the way he viewed himself. Being average had shaken his confidence every time he went out and saw the underwear models and firefighter calendars of the day. It seemed as though he would never be good enough for her, but she liked him. You could tell through the look she shot him every time he came into eyesight. It was one of those looks that could cut through a man's soul in a heartbeat. That look that where she raises her head slowly, slightly blinking, with the slightest of smiles gracing the contours of her face. There was no doubt that she cares for Steve, but Steve was too consumed with himself to realize.

After a while of milling about, Steve finally came to the realization that he forgot to talk to Roxy. So he pushed his way past a few family members stopping for a second to speak to his great-aunt Mildred who was weeping. When he finally reached her, she embraced him immediately. I was far away from them, but I could hear the conversation quite well,

"Hey there Roxanne, sad thing, eh?" I heard Steve say slight tinge in his throat from crying, "my brother always seemed like the angry one but I guess he truly loved her, did you hear about his letter? It was..." He paused as if to recall the words he wished to use, "exquisitely prepossessing"

Her voice seemed abnormally quiet for her, but that soft, supple voice still rang clear, "Yeah, I couldn't believe when I heard. He was such a sweetheart. In some ways, I would have liked a husband like him." As she said that I saw the look again. The look that said, "I'm hoping you notice me today." She also flung her hair off to the side so her face was clear. Something that Roxanne would do quite often when talking to Steve.

Completely oblivious, He continued on his spiel, tears welling up in his eyes, "I wish that he was still here so that he could teach me some things. He seemed to at least partially understand love, and women. I am just so...."

"So what? You are so depressing sometimes, I just don't know why you don't open your eyes and see what is right in front of you," she had tears in her eyes, not for her friend and fellow worker but for the love that Steve was constantly passing up. She shook her head in despair and turned to walk away. Steve stood there dumbfounded as to how the conversation had turned and he muttered to himself, "nice one."

As she turned I realized she was heading in my direction,

probably heading to the bathroom. I shifted even slightly more so that my face was hidden further. I knew I was well hidden between my hat and the relative shade of the plant, but I was still nervous because of my participation in this day. Though if she took a good look at me she would realize I was the man that she saw almost every day with different faces at different places. She would normally just pass me by, but the last few times she would stop to look at me as if she was having some sense of déjà vu. She stopped again as she was walking by she turned, her tear struck face twisted in pain. I couldn't help but look, for some reason I had a compassion for her and it was starting to show in more ways than one. She stood for a few seconds tears streaming down her face and then she turned to me.

"Stop!"

Chapter Two- of Dreams and Decisions

What could she have meant by that? There was no way she could have figured out my identity and it was highly unlikely that she recognized me from the street. Did it mean she knew of my intent to get her and Steve together? Maybe she was just screaming out for the world to hear like someone being overpowered by emotions they hate. Whatever the case, I couldn't risk sticking around. I started towards the doors through the meandering rivers of people.

There were a million thoughts that flooded my head. So many that they were beginning to overpower my mind, drowning out the dull roar of the mourning people around me. I needed to focus, to get some semblance of sanity back into a world shaken by one word. I left the church and sat down on the steps for a few seconds just to let the thoughts swim around. A panic slowly creeping through my body. The weather around me just adding to the morose atmosphere. I needed to calm myself but I couldn't control my musings.

Roxanne's simple statement piqued my curiosity. An image stapled to my mind refusing to give way to rational thought. I had the picture of her mascara running, her lipstick smudged from wiping her sleeve across her face, she had messed up hair from running her fingers through it. It was an image of sadness and I couldn't remove it. Not to say I didn't try. As I sat there on those steps, rain drenching me through all the layers of clothing, I tried to think of something, anything else. It just seemed as though her knowing made everything more terrifying and I was slowly becoming traumatized by that thought. I have hidden in the shadows for many a century. Ever since the 1600's when I was born. From the war waging period of industry to the technology fuelled modern era, I had never been caught. So it was abhorrent to think that my mark discovering me. Though more than anything it was her statement that ran through my mind. Like a haunting echo. "Stop..." that was all she said… "Stop". What does that mean? For the life of me, I could not figure it out.

    I got up from my well-worn spot on the stairs and made my way down the street towards my recently purchased town car. A black, four door, very basic looking vehicle glistening in the twilight and rain. It seemed only suitable that a man who normally wears a trench coat and follows people, meddling in their lives, would drive around in the car formally used by the FBI. They exited the building close to nine in the evening and over the course of the funeral, because of the mood, the weather had changed from sunny earlier in the day to a light drizzle. By the time the funeral ended that drizzle had turned into a downpour. Just as it always is, as if nature always knows when sad events are going on. Or it might be the Creator sending his condolences for their loss.

    After being to a few funerals, I had gotten the feeling that this was not merely speculation but that it was truth. Most of the time you would just hear the thunder roll through and hear the echo of each raindrop as they smashed into the ceiling above. It seemed like an almost magical sound when you are surrounded by dryness. A beautiful symphony of song to accompany the melancholy of the day. With the bass rumbling through to your soul and the melody touching every fibre of your being. Then once you left the safety of the building you would get to experience the calming feeling of water pouring over you, hugging you, and trying to console you.

When a person enters a funeral, they always have a mixture of emotions, the majority of which they cannot explain. When they leave, a static emotion is felt throughout. It's a type of sadness that cannot be described easily because the sorrow is like no other. The people leaving the service were distanced and lost as if they were waking up from a dream. A dream where their loved ones were fine and nothing had changed. Where they could laugh with them one more time, experience life with them just once more. When reality hits, it cripples them. They sink to the floor defeated. Broken and shattered, they walk out of the church disoriented with the pain that is so fresh inside of them. They all had the look of fake strength, the look they would lose when they returned home and once again dissolved into tears. You could often see past the charade when you saw the emptiness echoing in their eyes. It was a look that could bring sorrow to any man that might witness it.

Whatever the feeling, the mood was the same: sad. As the people filed out the sanctuary I caught a glimpse of Steve and Roxanne leaving together. Steve holding a dark blue umbrella over Roxanne's head. They both wore a faint smile on their faces. Out of place in the sea of straight, emotionless faces. The reason became apparent as they passed by my car. They had one of the pictures of Tom and I had to assume they were talking about his life. Those great memories they both shared. Like the time he accidentally got too drunk and started rambling to them about how great Sarah was. They walked towards a powder blue Volkswagen bug that was three vehicles behind me and hopped in.

Over the weeks, I realized this was Roxanne's preferred mode of travel. She believed that owning a car was still extremely practical even with the rising price of gas and her relatively long commute to work. Soon they zoomed past me, off to return Steve to his dwelling. I roared my vehicle to life to head back to my domicile for the night.

I had a simple home, downtown in a small city on the outskirts of a major city centre. I would never pay attention to names because of how often it seemed to me that I would move on to the next job. It was just a small apartment in the middle of all the stores that litter the street. A lot of people confused it for one of the places of business, often asking what I sold. I loved being surrounded by places of shop because everything I needed was right next door to me.

Unlike humans I didn't need food to nourish me, nor did I need to bathe in order keep clean. As a Loveless, I was granted certain freedoms normal humans didn't have. First was the ability to fly if there was a need for it. The wings slid right into the sockets that would be taken up by shoulder blades. They adorned my back as a nice decoration when I wasn't using them. With my shirt off people would just confuse them for perfectly rendered tattoos. However, they still raised off my back two inches so I needed to hide them with a corset. I preferred not using them because it was so easy to be spotted. I loved the feel of flying but, for me, they were only a nice bit of decoration on my body.

We were also granted immunity to aging stopping at the beautiful age of 23. We also had no imperfections of body and we could even avoid death through a natural regeneration process brought on by absorbing light just like a living solar panel. We had no technical bounds to our powers. We were near limitless provided we were in the light. Just a glimmer of light would empower us beyond belief. The darkness would counter those effects, seeping our powers out until we were weaker than a bug underfoot.

This could be easily remedied with a quick tear. A natural defense against the darkness that surrounded the globe. It was a bioluminescent entity that would shine brighter than a lantern. It was quite like a firefly that lights up the absence around them. This defense would allow us time to heal and fight back against any adversary that thought it wise to fight us. Of course, this was decided mainly based on if the Master saw us fit to behold such power. Should we fail to follow his commands for us we would lose those abilities. Often sending the Overseer, an angel, to correct us and reprimand us before dissecting our power by burning our wings off.

Our leader was called by many names from many societies. He was given an official name before the Creator sent him to Earth the first time. He introduces himself to many now as Gabriel. We referred to him as the Overseer seeing as that was his job. He was a very influential figure back in the past, proclaiming the words of the Master to many and letting people know of coming events. At one point he even told a man he was going to have a baby and that his wife wasn't cheating on him even though that would have been his natural thought.

Gabriel was able to make anyone fall in love with anyone else. At one point being called Cupid by the humans. Though he renounced working with the humans in that area when he was placed in leadership over the angelic ranks and the Loveless faction of the Resonance. It was back during the age of Jesus that we formed the society of the Faithless, knowing we would need to be there for the humans through this major shift in history. A few years later the hopeless were formed to take care of the morbid depression that hit during the dark ages. Finally, during the early nineteenth century, the Loveless were formed. Some Resonance decided not to work in any of their societies. Choosing rather to mill around the world doing nothing. I was that way until the Loveless was formed.

The Loveless followed a creed set forth by Gabriel. To make love what it should be. We have abided by this creed since the beginning and I vowed to keep it no matter how Hopeless the situation seemed. Love, however fleeting, was still out there. It was just that love was slowly deteriorating; disappearing faster than it was being formed. To be certain of how much was in the world was impossible. Though, when I was entrusted with Steve's relationship I was specifically told to not fail at any cost. I would try my hardest. Even if it took everything I was.

I opened the door to my house and shuffled to my bed through the small hallway separating the few rooms I had access to. I was exhausted after thinking through every possible outcome of Roxanne's words. It had been extremely dark since the rain had started. It was because of this fact that I fell asleep almost instantly after hitting the soft covers of my bed.

Then it started again, that dream that seeped into my fabric of reality each night. It always started the same, waking up in a new world that seemed so much different than ours. Even though it was oddly familiar. Like a memory that had faded into oblivion, only to resurface for slight moments throughout daily life, making us think we had already experienced it.

As I looked around, I took account of the subtle differences in the atmosphere. A picture here, a light switch there, but it was always the same building. This time, a picture was crooked. Tilted as if the house were on an angle and the picture thought it was upright. Other than that it was the same hallway, the same couches, the same carpet poking through the gaps between my toes. Every detail so perfect, yet imaginary.

After walking around in the dream and sitting on the couches I had gotten used to, I realized something was up. The faceless girl who normally called out to me was missing. Usually, she was missing for the first hour or so during sleep. I had discovered this after waking up one of the times right after she appeared and looking at my clock. This time, I could feel that her presence wasn't there. I couldn't hear her voice; hear her footsteps on the hardwood floors; see fleeting images of her or any of the normal occurrences that had become routine for my dreams.

Then I heard it, that haunting voice cascading down the hallway echoing off the walls. A beautiful voice that couldn't be matched to anyone I had come into contact with. I expected those sweet words she would always say, "Welcome home," but instead the words came in like a rushing wind, knocking the air out of my lungs and crushing the reality of the dream,

"STOP!"

What could this mean? Was this faceless woman I had continually dreamt about actually Roxanne? The plights of the day had seeped into my dream and I needed an answer. So I asked myself the only question I felt needed, "What should I stop?"

Once again that voice echoed throughout the imaginary realm, "STOP, JUST STOP!" it was with this that I startled awake. Drenched in sweat, I just sat there for a few minutes listening to my alarm buzzing. I felt the sweat drip down my forehead as I tried to get up. Roxanne's words seemed like they would haunt me forever. Creeping into every facet of my life. I put it out of my mind and continued on to my day.

Getting dressed always seemed to be a struggle for me. My wings would always get caught in my shirt, so I started using a corset to keep them in place. Even though they hid well in my back they were still cumbersome and burdensome when wearing human clothing. It didn't hurt quite as much as I would have thought since my wings would just conform to the contours of the corset being that they are composed of light. The real hassle was finding something that would shade over my face enough that no human could see it.

My face was beyond beautiful compared to most humans, so hiding it was the only way to make sure people didn't notice me. Sure I could shift my face to look different but that took a lot of energy and that was not something I liked to do. The last girl that saw my face fell in love with me, which was a problem since I couldn't love her back. I had to move away from that job because she started to stalk me. It was all I could do to keep myself from going insane.

I slipped on a pair of blue jeans that conformed to the curves of my leg and put on the trench coat I had become accustomed to wearing. I topped off the uniform with a rustic cowboy hat that tied the image together. Today would begin the Process. A seven-step program developed by Gabriel in order to help us. This first step was simple, show the man how beautiful the girl was. Most men have an innate sense of beauty from the moment they're born. So it is normally pretty easy for a man to see that in a woman. Dress her up with a bit of make-up and she would knock him dead. This was necessary because of physical attraction. If a man is not physically attracted to a woman then they have the opportunity to look elsewhere. They then fall into the trap of the world saying that there might be someone better. More times than not, they fall for it. That was the difficulty of this step: Proving her to be more beautiful than anyone else. In Roxanne's case, this would be easy considering her natural charm.

As I left the house I heard that echoing voice once more. At first, I thought that it was a coincidence, just a remnant of the dream, but as I continued waking up I realized it couldn't have been. Dreams are based on the subconscious. That means you need to be unconscious, not thinking, or asleep in order to dream. At that moment, I wasn't any of the above. I considered the fleeting possibility that the voice might haunt me forever but I dismissed that thought as quickly as it came.

As the car spurred to life I thought through the plan for the day. It started with finding Steve. Of course, with all the power at our disposal, we cannot just find a person. We have to look for them. Luckily, Steve followed a pretty routine schedule. He got up early, at around ten in the morning, and would drive to the local Starbucks. He would then acquire a *Venti Mocha Frappuccino* without whipping crème. Then he would then sit for an hour sipping at his drink every so often while reading the morning news.

Departing, he would go to the local diner to sit in for a burger. After that, it was anyone's guess. Due to spontaneity and never having a static job he might be anywhere. This also wasn't helped by the fact that he was constantly in and out of relationships. Never with the same girl for more than two weeks.

The process of finding him would take anywhere from fifteen minutes to an hour each day. The most difficult aspect of the day would be when I caught up with him. Following someone was easy, but doing it in a way that hid your presence was ridiculously difficult. This was even more important considering the turn of events that had befallen me. Having both of my subjects knowing of my presence was not a thought I wanted to entertain. So I took to some extra precautions. After reaching the local Starbucks I parked the car and decided to take a cab to the diner since Steve wasn't working his way through his drink.

As we were driving we pulled up behind a Buick Enclave with Steve's license plate and I knew I had caught up with him. I entrusted the cabbie with the job of following, discreetly, behind Steve to wherever he was going. I knew it would be the diner, but it was better to be safe than sorry. My paranoia was starting to resurface again when I noticed Steve looking back a few times. Just to be safe I asked the cabbie to pull over to the side of the road.

I exited the cab and paid the driver the fee with a twenty-dollar tip. I quickly stretched and then made the short jaunt over to the diner. As the cabbie drove away I noticed a smile on his face. Just another one of the flawed humans that loved money more than humanity. Well, as much as it was distressing, I couldn't do anything about him. He wasn't my mark though I would love to have seen him fall in love with his mate that was prepared specifically for him. All these thoughts flooded my head as I walked down the pathway towards Jeni's Diner. A cute 50's remake diner just off the main avenue in town. It was a good tourist trap.

I entered the diner and was greeted by the chirp of a small bell. Its sound would always incite joy in my heart. I took a quick account of the restaurant and noticed Steve sitting in his regular spot. The third booth on the left-hand side of the establishment. To my providence, a booth was open just behind that booth. I had a chance to begin the Process now. All I needed was an opening.

"Could you get me a double-double and a jalapeño burger, thanks, Janet." Steve asked as Janet took down his order.

I opened my mouth to start talking but was interrupted mid-attempt, "could I take your order sir," Janet, with her cleavage exposed, had just bounced up to my table. Her bubbly personality overflowing and filling the diner with a special kind of happiness. She was relatively small with pixie cut blond hair and in her diner outfit, she was a sight to behold. I sat there for a while admiring her beauty while she waited for me to order. After a bit of an awkward silence, she sheepishly said, "would you like to know what the special of the day is?"

I sounded out without thinking, "same as him." I put up my thumb and motioned to Steve. I knew he had heard and I could hear him rustling around in his seat. He was turning around; my worst fear had been realized: I was going to have to have a conversation with him. I heard the rough drone of his voice say to me, "hey, a man with good taste, names Steve, what's yours?"

I couldn't comprehend how within a period of two days I had been, seemingly, revealed to both of my marks. I was at a loss as to how I was slipping so badly. I sat there in the booth reeling with the possibilities of how to get out of the situation. I realized my pause and answered him, "my name is Cornelius and my last name doesn't matter. I just enjoy the same thing." I had an opportunity now but I had to play it well. If I was too eager, he might think something was up. If I'm too cold to the situation, he may lose interest.

He seemed to contemplate something before answering and just plainly stating, "ok nice to meet you, have a great meal. This place is just great I come here every day!" He was completely oblivious. I was able to relax a bit and I used the opportunity to begin working on the Process.

"This place is pretty great," I said, "I come here to think. Which

I've needed to do a lot lately. Started going out with this girl and I just can't get her out of my mind. Can you relate?" I shifted slightly so he knew I was interested in a bit of a conversation.

He turned and looked at me with a dead blank stare. A look of contemplation crossing his face as the gears in his head started moving. He hunched over a bit leaning in as if he had a secret and said, "The most beautiful girl in the world is named Roxanne. However, every time I try to get close to her she shuts me out. That isn't your issue, though..." He trailed off as he completed the thought. Utterly defeated and broken from years of unsuccessful battles with himself over the same issue.

He did like her but for some reason, he believed that she didn't like him. It was painfully obvious from every interaction that she liked him. She even told him so on a few occasions in a round about manner. Steve's view on Roxanne was so flawed. He had so many doubts and you could see them weighing on his shoulders as he sat there. I thought quickly about what I could say to him. I leaned in a bit further and said, "Just look for the signs, maybe she does like you."

He seemed dismayed by this comment but said quite calmly, "that'll be the day." With that, I knew the conversation was over. He shifted back in his seat awaiting his burger. I had successfully completed the first step without even trying but that meant it was only going to get harder. Next I had to break him out his depressive mindset. Though, I didn't quite understand why he thought the way he did. Why was he so set on the fact that she didn't like him? I needed to find out what happened in their past. There had to be something, some small little detail I missed when I first took the case. Steve felt inadequate and there was always an answer for that.

People's viewpoints of love often seemed to be passed down from their parents. The little idiosyncrasies that the parents would have more often than not transferred to their kids. It was the mixture between two parents raised fairly well that would lead to the couple being good parents themselves. This was why most girls, even though they have the urge too, would never tell a guy straight out that she liked him. For the same reason, it is why guys never believed they are good enough for the girl of their dreams. It was a feeling that was passed on from generation to generation.

I followed him for the rest of the day, going from monotonous task to dreary chore as he went about working, all the while thinking about our short conversation. I knew his past quite well and I was certain there was nothing to dissuade him from a relationship. He had known Roxanne since grade two. They quickly became friends and would hang out a lot in their high school years. Roxanne then dated other guys but would always include Steve and Steve just didn't date. Every time that Roxanne would break up with a guy she would come running to Steve to have him console her. After high school, Steve went to the University of Alberta and Roxanne followed getting a full-time job with a big conglomerate in Edmonton. Then after Steve had finished his law degree he moved to a small city called Innisfail. There he started up a small law firm with his brother, Tommy and associates.

Roxanne left her job in Edmonton just as she was about to get promoted to assistant manager. She did this in order to be close to Steve. Everything checked out. There wasn't anything in my recent memory that could have made him so depressive about the situation. So why did he feel that way? Everything that had happened that day had set my mind spinning. A massive collection of confusion and data that jumbled together to make a mess. I would figure out why he thought the way he did. Then I remembered that voice, "STOP." As if being called from the deepest annals of my memory. Screeching out to be heard through the mire of the day. Maybe she was trying to warn me. How could she know though? My general conclusion was that I had been looking at her with compassion and she didn't want anything to do with that. That comforted me for a bit.

I fell asleep after the long day of following Steve thinking about the fact that I normally go home before Steve goes to work. I knew that the next day would consist of scrounging through old files and newspaper articles hoping to find some semblance of an answer. I had more information than I knew what to do with. It would be a grueling process, but I knew it had to be done. If only to find why his feelings are so flawed.

As my head hit the pillow and the shadow of sleep began to overwhelm me I felt a serene peace. Something I hadn't felt since the dreams had started. As my eyes fluttered shut I thought to myself. Why am I so calm tonight? I know I'm going to dream of *her* again...

Chapter Three- Of Days Gone by and Discoveries

But I didn't. That night I didn't dream. I lay restlessly thinking about their past. Restlessly playing out every move in my mind searching for any incident that might have started a feeling of unworthiness on Steve's part. The longer I lay in the bed, the worse I felt. Feeling every odd curvature of the bed underneath me. Soon it was just too overwhelming, so I got up to begin my search for information. I began walking towards my study stopping only to look at the clock above the mantle. It read 4:38 in the morning. I had enough time that I could do a large amount of research and still be able to get out there and scout out the relationship. I dressed very nonchalantly knowing that no one could see me inside of my domicile. Electing to wear a loose housecoat with slots in the back for my wings to fly free. It felt good to have a bit of freedom, if only for a few hours.

I got into my study and looked around at the randomized chaos. There were boxes full of news articles from the past cities they had been in. Books on love languages and psychological studies. A small, mahogany desk was the centrepiece of the room with stacks of papers of various sizes and colors littered all over. It had been over four months since I had started the research stage and even in all that time I couldn't have looked through all the resources.

There were literally thousands of records to go through. Even if I took a few months to study I still wouldn't dent the innumerable assets I had gained. I needed to continue searching if I had any inclination of finding the cause for Steve's disconsolate attitude towards Roxanne. I figured the High School age would be the most logical area to begin. I made my way over to a haphazardly stacked pile of boxes marked 1998-2008. One of the many markings throughout the room. I opened up the top box and began removing article after article.

One of the many reasons they were such good friends was because they had attended the same High School. Grade ten was awkward for their relationship. It was the beginning of their respective voyages into dating. Specifically, Roxanne's voyages into dating. The first guy Roxanne went out with was an outlier in the school. Known widely for being an outcast. It seemed to everyone that it was pity that caused her to go out with him. They dated for the better part of four months before Roxanne was abruptly let go from her aspect of the relationship. Everyone's view of the relationship was wrong. Roxy went immediately to Steve to break down. She wept for hours until finally giving into sleep. Steve, of whom I received all of this information from listening in on conversations, didn't mind since she slept on him until the next day.

After that Steve started to take an interest in women, noticing their beauty but never capitalizing on his opportunities. In one such instance the head cheerleader, a beach blond babe, attempted to break Steve's barrier but was abruptly shut down. This hit school headlines as she became very irate. It was relatively clear that Steve intended to save himself for Roxy and her alone. I chuckled to myself as I read the article on the cheerleader. Realizing how ridiculous it was that he denied every feasible attempt women made on him and Roxy would not. Though every time a relationship ended she would go running to Steve and sleep in his arms that night as a permanent solution for being consoled.

Roxanne's longest relationship was with Bobby Thoron, the quarterback. A beefy 17-year-old with a strong chiselled jaw and a well-defined system of muscles. They were often the talk of the town as, aesthetically, they were the most beautiful combination in the school. She stayed with the adonis for a year and two months before someone more beautiful moved to the school and Thor moved on. During that entire year, Steve retained hope and would often invite himself along on their dates. Which consistently disagreed with Thoron's jealous temperament. Roxanne often having to step in and calm the zealous pair.

It was about an hour and a half into my escapade when something caught my eye, a small comment on a note I had taken from the early days of following Roxanne. It happened on the third of June 2007, two weeks before their grade twelve prom. Apparently, according to a conversation between Roxy and a girlfriend of hers, Steve had approached Roxanne about going with him. It was there she had rejected him for the first time. After that, he seemed to distance himself more as if accepting a false reality that she truly hated him. This just was not the case, during that period Roxy's family had lost a lot of money and she didn't have the money for a prom dress. Because of this, she didn't accept his proposal. This small overlooked detail, the most insignificant of events, had started Steve on the path to denial.

It couldn't have stopped there though. That would be impossible, for one event to have caused such strong feelings of rejection. I got up and stretched walking around for a bit to shake out the stubbornness in my muscles. I went into the kitchen and prepared a small breakfast and ate it quickly while looking at the paper that had been delivered to me a couple of days earlier. Then I returned to study and continued rummaging through the records. This time moving through the records surrounding Steve's college years.

Steve came from a privileged family so going to the University of Alberta didn't cost him anything, however, Roxanne came from the middle class, often struggling to make ends meet, so she was unable to afford university. She wanted to stay close to Steve and so she found an apartment that was cheap. A shabby shack that could barely be considered a home for homeless people. It had four walls and a roof, though, so it was good enough for her. She also found a well-paying job that she excelled at. Moving up the ranks quickly within the first few months.

Steve would be in school a good twelve hours every day. When he wasn't in school he was either studying or hanging out with Roxanne. She would always be at his disposal and even gave up some of her work in order to visit with him. Roxanne was often chastised for this, but would always do her job so well that it made up for the work that she missed.

Over the next two years, she became a head journalist of the local newspaper while Steve had gone through his courses with a 3.9 GPA. Steve had impressed the law community so much with his knowledge that he was invited out to a few court cases to watch and, in some cases, participate in. One newspaper article laid out his first case, a divorce suit between Tom and Sarah De'Lemit. It was a two-month case in which the outcome was excruciatingly painful. As a student, he had no choice in persons whom he would represent. Steve was assigned to Sarah and through a grueling process, he won the case. This allowed Steve to continue to move up through the ranks. He gained a reputation quite quickly. Within the next three months after his first case, he won three more cases, one of which was against an attempted murder suspect. Though he was still in school he was becoming one of the best lawyers in Edmonton.

Through all of this, he worked hard on his friendship with Roxy. Every chance he would get, he would sneak off and see her. They did not date though, just hang out together. It seemed like they were constantly getting closer. I saw no reason why he would have this thought that she didn't like him. In fact, it seemed like he had completely forgotten about her denial at prom. So now I was at square one again. So I began to look through the cases that Steve had been given.

The first few were divorce cases then an attempted murder case, a few stolen identity cases, a B&E, two robbery cases one for each side, and finally a fraud case with a small time business. I took a quick glance through each case hoping to find something there. Everything seeming normal, as I looked through the outline of each one. All I saw was a lot of depravity and soul-wrenching cases. Then I came about to the attempted murder case and a name jumped off the page. Roxanne Gersch. The article said:

MOTHER ALMOST KILLED BY PSYCHO FATHER.

Amanda Gersch, mother of Roxanne Gersch was recently attacked by her husband of twenty-one years. The man, Jarrod Gersch, took a knife and slashed his wife three times in the throat and once in the stomach. Amanda was rushed to the hospital and was in critical condition for forty-three hours. After she was in stable condition a lawsuit was placed. Steve De'Lemit, a student in the law course at the University of Alberta was the plaintiff's attorney. The accused was placed in prison with a sentence of 5 years to life. When asked to comment Roxanne stated, "He should have got so much more than just twenty years: he almost killed my mother. He should be in there till he rots." Amanda said in a short conversation in her hospital room, "He gets what he deserves, but I still feel bad that he didn't get more. The law system is very flawed like that."

Reading that seemed to fit with this feeling of inadequacy that haunted Steve. Sure, he was able to win the case, but he couldn't give Roxanne, and her mom, the peace they wanted. They knew they would have a very violent man out of prison too early after the incident. If this truly was the cause for his discouraged attitude, then it would be easy to correct. He just had to know that she had forgiven him for what he had done. That would cure his little quirk.

When I finally looked up, I saw that it was one in the afternoon. I had missed my chance to learn more about Steve for the day. All that was left was to set up a plan. Normally my approach was simple: go in, implant ideas, and leave. But the fact that I was certain both Roxanne and Steve knew, even in a relative sense, who I was put a flaw in that plan. I had to be more subtle, if not more for the sake of my safety, than for the sake of the mission. I had decided that it wasn't worth worrying about. I was going to approach this case directly. Befriending them as much as possible. Even if that went against everything I had learned.

In the long run, I still had more research to do. So I kept looking into it. After a quick nap, I resumed reading through their past. After the lawsuits their friendship seemed to disappear slowly. They still spent time together, but it was more spread out, and it was never for hours on end. They were becoming more like colleagues than anything else. It continued like this for almost four months after the lawsuit.

After that leeway period, they started to hang out more often again. It seemed as though she had gotten used to the fact that Steve couldn't do anything about the time her dad was going to be in prison. A tension remained though, straining the once great friendship. Steve wouldn't spend time alone with Roxanne anymore only seeing her at larger gatherings. She had forgiven him, but he couldn't forgive himself. At least, it seemed that way.

It was then that I started to see a pattern in some of the photos. A few mysterious figures in the background, never in the foreground. The first man was a tall figure, brooding and malicious. Slightly built and always hidden behind other people. In the shadows, but there he was none the less.

I had seen them before, back near the beginning of the Resonance's escapade into love. They were fallen Resonance, the exact opposite of our society in every way. A lot like the true Fallen who followed the First Fallen in the beginning. Where we proclaim the image and direct essence of the Master, they show the idiosyncratic nature of the First fallen. Pure evil essence walking around in broken Resonance bodies. Often when a Resonance breaks the rule against love they will go and work for the First Fallen.

The more photos I looked at, the more I saw these impure beings. They were following both Steve and Roxanne. I noticed three different creatures that appeared throughout the many photos scattered about my desk. The tall one would often dress in ancient garb, wearing colonial English outfits. He was the only one whose face was clearly visible. The rest were shrouded in darkness. On each of them, I could clearly make out two piercing red eyes. A deep red that matched the color of fresh blood.

The second was relatively short compared to the other two. He didn't have any features about him that immediately stood out to me but I knew he was a part of the Dissenters, a group of Resonance who left because of personal difference. I could tell because of the cloud of darkness that hovered around his figure. An unnatural lighting that seemed to suck the brightness from every picture that he was a part of. I could sense an evil presence seeping out the photo changing the atmosphere of the room.

Finally, the third, brutish figure, showed up often side by side with one of his compatriots. He was large, beyond natural standards, like a tree that had gained the ability to move. Every part of his body was unnaturally large. This was only exaggerated by the extenuating anorexic standard of his partners. It often seemed as though he was the leader of the other two and was often pictured leaning over and speaking to them.

As I looked through the fourteen or so photos I had picked them out of, I heard a loud crashing sound coming from behind me. I turned, quickly getting to my feet to investigate the disturbance. I slinked out of my study looking in each room along the hallway making my way towards the door. I pulled my wings into my back and shifted my face in case there was someone inside the house. Each room I looked in seemed unnaturally still, a paranoia creeping into my subconscious as I considered it being the followers of the First fallen. I had heard rumours that they could sense when someone was thinking of them but that was just a myth. No creature the Master creates had the ability to read others minds, lest they equal the power of the Creator. It was ridiculous to think otherwise.

I made my way into my living area where I surveyed the scene. Everything was pristine other than a broken pot and dirt that had sprayed in an arc from the crash site. One of my plants had fallen from a windowsill pushed by the wind. I breathed a sigh of relief and turned to return to my study pausing for a second as a chill spread down my spine. I ignored it and continued back to studying for a few more hours before turning in for the day.

I entered the room and made my way to one of the bookshelves that lined the walls. There were numerous blue bound books that lined the shelves. Each one a direct copy of the last with gold lettering written down the spine. I pulled out the fourth from the end and opened it to where a small, red, linen strap had been placed. I read over the last page and pulled out a quill. Dipping into an inkwell that was sitting on the desk, I began writing. Another entry in a journal that I had been keeping since the beginning of my work as a Loveless.

> *"24th of September 2016 (A.D.),*
>
> *I learned some interesting things about the couple today; they seem to be strong together. However, the insecurities of Steve are beyond me. His fear is beyond my comprehension. There have only been two incidents I have found that could even implicate that he should have this inferiority complex. Other than that, Roxanne has presented herself before him as something he should take. She seems to be throwing herself at him and he is too stupid to catch her.*
>
> *It will be a challenge to get these two together but I truthfully believe that with enough planning and strictly following the rules and steps to love it may be able to happen. I cannot fail, I will not fail."*

I knew then that I was invested. I had an emotional connection to these people, I cared for them. Also, I knew that if I failed now love, as we all knew it, would disappear. There might be fleeting glimpses of love but never the purity of true love that can never be broken. Roxanne had true love. She displayed it by following Steve wherever he would go, forgiving him whenever he failed. She wanted to love him and it seemed like nothing would tear that love apart. She was a beautiful woman and she could have pursued any man, but she chose him.

In all of their time together Steve had a twinge of doubt that had become a full blown reason for running away. I knew he could come around, I had seen it before. Two cases ago I had a couple that dealt in a similar circumstance. Their names, Deloris and Don Fents. Don was forty years old going through a mid-life crisis. Deloris was a girl who liked things to be set out and under her complete control. When Don started to change himself, Deloris backed away from the relationship. She couldn't handle his change so she just packed up and left.

I helped them rekindle their relationship but it was never the same. Don had become juvenile, acting like a ruthless teen. Deloris had become a bitter and vile old lady and when the pair returned to their relationship they couldn't do anything other than fight. Eventually, this led to them seeing other people and I knew that I had lost that case. I had worked with Don and had changed his mind slightly through suggestion. It was not enough.

I couldn't have that happen with Steve and Roxanne. It would break my heart into a thousand pieces to see a love so true ruined by the simplest of problems. It broke my heart back then and it would still break it now. I wouldn't let something like that happen. I couldn't. I had to succeed. No matter what.

I flipped a few pages back in my diary and started to read the first entry, just to see what I thought of Steve and Roxanne when I first started to help them,

"11th of July 2016 (A.D.),

Today I met Steve and Roxanne, the subjects of my next endeavour. I was tasked to precipitate a relationship with this couple and Gabe made it seem

to be of utmost importance. As I left he told me,

"No matter what happens you have to keep going with this couple. You cannot fail!"

I have failed before and there is the eternal possibility of me failing again.

The rest of the Loveless have been told to remain in the strongholds and I'm not quite certain why. I am guessing it is to keep them from losing their powers. To limit the depravity creeping through our ranks. Too many are falling out of our society, it is quite sad. I wasn't going to lose my powers now, even though I feel that I will break some rules with this couple. I can sense it.

This couple seems like a straight forward case. He likes her, she likes him. He considers her paradisiacal. It is Simple enough to get them together though she seems to look at me like she recognizes me every time that I pass by her. I can only take this with a spoon full of salt, though. I have thought the couple I was to bring together knew me before and it turned out they thought I was a Sherlock Holmes character. Someone from a comic convention. At least, that's what I heard them say. I couldn`t read too much into it.

Anyways I guess writing a journal is hard. I have told myself to write in this every day and I am missing so many days. I guess it happens though so I am going to just keep trying to write down information about the couple. Hopefully, this is just an open and shut case."

How wrong I was back then. This was not an open and shut case and for all I knew Roxanne actually knew who I was and Steve had some semblance as well. It was now clear to me that I needed to reveal myself to them as a friend to get them together.

I looked up at the clock again and was shocked when I saw that it was already eight in the evening. I left the study taking one last look at the mass of information. I walked to my room and dropped onto the bed with force ready to be overtaken by the realm of my subconscious. I slipped into unconscious within a few minutes. Fully prepared to be taken by my nightmares.

Chapter Four- Of Defining Times and Deepening Relations

I awoke in a fret, panting as if I had just finished running a marathon. An echo of a voice long gone ringing in my ears as my body woke up. It was the same dream again, with the new addition of her haunting statement. Her features similar to the past nights with the exception of a slim, button nose that appeared in the middle of the featureless face. I had tried before to draw a picture of this vision before, but every time failed to capture the surrealism of it. I sat on the side of my bed for a few seconds with my head in my hands contemplating the involuntary dream. I shook my head and got up, ready to begin anew with the job I loved. I had taken a day to recover from studying and to process the mass of information that I had sifted through. Though, I was ready to get out and continue pressing Steve and Roxy together.

As I set out for the day I realized how much easier my approach would be without having to hide from them. I kept my distance from Steve though and I had noticed that he didn't seem to be looking over his shoulder like he was the last time I had gone out to follow him. When we finally reached the diner he didn't notice me walk in after him and assume my seat behind him. Just as I sat down I heard the familiar triad of bells that marked Steve getting a phone call. I heard him flip open his old fashioned phone and say the familiar, "olla!" almost immediately changing his voice once he recognized the caller. His voice softened and smoothed ever so slightly as he said, "oh hey, been a few days, how ya' doing?"

I could only hear murmuring from the phone itself and it was indistinguishable. From the way Steve was talking I assumed that it was

Roxanne. She was the only one he would speak to in such a relaxed manner. Often Steve took to being regal and stoic in the way that he spoke. His conversation seemed pretty disjointed without knowing the other half of the conversation. I kept hearing him say things like, "We should meet up in the near future," and "That is pretty spectacular," and then his voice dropped its enthusiasm. There was a shift in the atmosphere as everything seemed to follow the change in tone of voice. There were no words for a while as he listened to the mysterious personage on the other end of the line. After the prolonged period of silence, I heard him say almost monotonously, "Man, that's great... I hope you two are happy together. I guess I'll chat with you later Roxanne."

The phone clicked shut and I heard Steve sigh. He seemed distraught and when I looked toward the other side of the diner I saw his reflection in one of the chrome plates that were littered all over the place. He had his head on the table, exasperated from this unforeseen circumstance. What little hope he had of attaining a relationship with Roxanne had slipped away from his grasp. I heard him mutter under his breath, "well, that's it I guess."

This placed a bit of a kink in my plan. I hadn't accounted for Roxanne finding another man, or that they would have eyes for anyone but each other. I had a contingency plan in case something like this ever happened but it was not ideal. I knew of someone in the society who could make any man fall in love with her. Not because of a natural beauty or anything of that sort. Rather she did it through an almost magical charm that she exuded. One of her special powers that the light provided her. I just hoped she would be willing to help.

I heard rustling from Steve's booth and I noticed him getting up to leave. I moved slightly in my booth to hide for another day. I didn't need to begin that process with all of the other pressing matters taking precedence. As he left I noticed Janet come up to him and she asked if everything was all right. He just shrugged and said, "I guess things aren't meant to be. Just dealing with some personal issues, you know?" Janet nodded and accepted the payment for his meal. She smiled and went about her business as usual.

He had given up completely. No sense of hope left in the few words he spoke to Janet. I still had faith in their relationship. Love would always exist as long as they work towards each other. This might even give them an opportunity to get close again. When this guy leaves Roxanne, if he does, she would go running to Steve, like she had every other time, and, capitalizing on the situation, I could push them even closer.

I just had to follow the Process from there. The steps were simple enough; first, have a natural attraction. Some aspect of the other person that they found admirable and that they could be attracted to. Alongside this is the idea of a relationship. Both parties should want to be dating. If neither feels ready for a relationship, a forced one would break them apart more than before. In most cases that I had accepted it was cookie cutter. They could both find something in each other and they both had inclinations of relationships in their minds. In some cases, like Steve's, one of the pair would have to redevelop their feelings for the other. This would only take a bit of time but most men are rapidly forgiving when they know they have a lady truly interested in them.

Following that attraction came the personality stage. A stage meant to discover all of the quirks and idiosyncrasies that made up their own temperaments. Usually, this meant learning something new about the other person. I had seen many different occurrences of this over the years from little nonsensical things to huge secrets they had never told anyone else. In one such instance, a client had told his mark about breaking off a previous engagement in order to be with her. She reacted poorly, at first, seeing as it seemed like he would be willing to cheat on her, but she eventually grew to love the sacrifice that he had made for her.

The third, step was one of the hardest. It involved the man taking a leap of faith and introducing himself to his girlfriend's parents. This was often the hardest aspects because of the reluctance, on the man's part, of meeting people he was unfamiliar with. In society, it seemed like meeting the parents was something they did only after they started dating. However, it was of utmost importance to meet the parents before anything official begins in order to get some affirmation that this would be a right course of action. If they don't react well, they may see something that might cause a break in the relationship. Parents being all the more receptive to those sorts of signals.

After they meet the parents they would move on to longing. To long for someone is so much more than just wanting them to be close. It is awaiting every word, every footstep, every waking moment that you can be by their side. It is a feeling deep inside the chambers of your heart that urge you to continue on in any endeavour that would bring you closer to your significant other. Much like a magnetic connection that pulled two objects into a bond that cannot be broken. With this longing comes the beginning of the dating period.

Dating, in this process, is like putting superglue between two of the most powerful magnets and placing them in a vat of cement. It is the bonding process that would complete the myriad of emotions that they would be going through. In this place, through many dates, they would fall in love. Deep, powerful, unending love. It's the time that they spend together in this period experiencing this raw emotion that seals the relationship as pure. This love would continue growing until it reached the pinnacle of its existence, true love.

This true love would be formed in step six. This consisted of an act of courage on the part of the male. One that terrifies and incapacitates many. It involved him finding a beautiful setting in the most romantic place he could think of. Often trying to outdo every other date they had been on. It would also involve him finding a monetary token of their love. A physical manifestation of the feeling that he so cherished inside of him. A small metallic ring with diamonds covering its face. He would take his soulmate to this place and romance her. Bringing it to a moment where he would kneel down and as a sign of complete abandon he would ask her to be his wife.

Step seven is the outcome of all of the work combined in one celebration of love. A marriage ceremony. A marriage, which by all definitions, is eternal. It was something that lasted forever and that would only be broken by a false love that was rushed through the process, often skipping steps. This was why so many marriages end in divorce and why so many more deal with abuse, dissatisfaction, and in some cases even death. The final step would encourage them to stay together forever.

We were given the Process in a guidebook we called the Codex. We all knew the rules but because of the degeneration of love we had turned these easy seven steps into a million. Every date mattered, every word, every single moment. In the Resonance society all that matter was the physical aspect of the relationship. The ten minutes of pleasure and years of regret. That is why love was disappearing; it was becoming too complicated. It was the same with religion. Love had also become a hindrance to most people, getting in the way of their pursuit of money, fame, or happiness. I always found it funny that they passed up true happiness that lasted forever for a happiness that lasted until it was all used up.

I decided that I was going to go and "visit" Roxanne. See how she was doing with what I assumed was a new boyfriend. It was possible that she was just trying to make Steve jealous, but in any case, I had to find a way to split them up. Although, I absolutely despised destroying any form of happiness. Too many people suffer for so many reasons and just the thought of being one of those reasons hurt. I knew what my job was, and I knew her happiness would be found with Steve long before it would be found with whoever she was with now.

I had driven around much of the town looking in the major date locations. Even passing by her abode to see if Roxy was there. I had spent a half hour just driving when I saw her car parked outside of one of the fancier restaurants in town. A large well lit building along the main drag. It had large front windows that allowed the viewing public to see in on the romantic atmosphere inside. A wafting smell of French cuisine emanating out of the building. I looked at the sign and chuckled to myself. The restaurant was called C'est L'amour which meant "Love it" both describing the emotion felt towards the food and the atmosphere they were trying to encapsulate. It also sounded a bit like "say no more" which would be what they would say after the meal.

I parked my vehicle on the south side of the building and walked around to the front. Upon entering I was assaulted with the smell of

Coquilles Saint-Jacques, a great pastry dish, Boudin Noir Aux Pommes, an apple dish, and a very strong scent of wine. It was a heavenly smell and I was more than happy to give my business to this establishment. After waiting for a while in the reception area I heard a particularly bubbly voice say, "Why, hello stranger, do you have a reservation?"

I turned towards the voice and saw Janet was standing in front of me behind a small desk. Her figure was completely covered by a loose fitting waiter's garb. Almost like a suit. I quickly stopped admiring her and said, "No, I'll just wait for an open table." She cocked her head a bit and chuckled,

"It'll be a few minutes. Take a seat."

While waiting for the table I had time to think about my approach to breaking them up. I knew I would have to use my resource, but to convince her would be hard. We hadn't been on speaking terms for a few years and she harbored what could only be resentment for me. I pieced together an apology, just in case, and thought about where she might be hiding. I landed upon a brothel on the south side of the city which is where I had seen her last. It was an old Loveless stronghold that had long gone unoccupied. A few Loveless would use it as a headquarters when they were in the city on assignment but for the most part, it was unused.

After a short time of waiting, Janet came up and said, "We have a table waiting for you!" On the way to the table, I couldn't help but ask her, "Don't you work at the diner?"

"Yeah, but times are rough and I need the money to finish my degree so I work here as well. I also do my schooling during the evenings."

"Well, I admire your dedication to college but when do you

sleep?"

"Never," she laughed.

"What are you taking?"

"Religious sciences, with a minor in psychology and music but my passion is truly taking care of flowers..."

I saw the empty table ahead and decided to end the conversation there. It was interesting to me that there were still people so wholly dedicated to pursuing a proper education that they would work themselves ragged to pay for it. I smiled at her as I sat down and received the menu from her. She bounced away swinging her body in step with some rhythm in her head. An image of happiness and beauty.

I wanted to help her pay for college but I knew that the Loveless wouldn't look too highly on that use of finances. I would tip her highly, though, to give her a bit of a boost of support. I wanted her to succeed in her life, and anyway that I could help, I would.

As I looked around the open concept restaurant I noticed Roxanne sitting two tables away. She was in just the right position that I couldn't see the guy she was with. I listened to all the conversations going on around me and heard many different things. One man talking about an endeavor he hoped to complete in the New Year, another talking to her friend about a recent divorce, and many "couples" talking to each other about their "amazing lives". I also heard Roxanne's tale-tell laugh coming from her table. A slight combination of a light giggle and a riotous chortle.

After about an hour I could tell Roxanne was losing interest and wanted to get out of there. She was obviously bored as apparent by her constant looking around and checking her watch. I couldn't see much of her suitor but every so often I would see a large pudgy hand shoot out and grab another piece of escargot from the plate that sat between them.

After another half hour, I noticed Roxanne getting up to leave. She was dressed in a simple black dress that accentuated the curvature of her body. Her hair curled and teased to perfection. When she moved out of her chair I caught a glimpse of her date and recognized him immediately. It was Bobby Thoron, all grown up. Still wearing his vintage football jacket and proudly boasting two provincial championship rings on his right hand. His overall stature being bigger than the photo's I had seen of him from the past.

I asked for a check from Janet and, after giving her a two-hundred-dollar tip, left. I wouldn't be going back home quite yet. I had one more stop. I was going to Southside Haven; a development that was one of the oldest in the city. In the middle of that development was a building that was run down and dirty. It was the stronghold we had dubbed Backdoor Haven. It was now, for all intents and purposes, a strip club used by the general public. In the back was the entrance to the stronghold, a secret door nobody knew about leading to an underground city that used to house many of the Resonance. I was going to get Bobby Thoron a girlfriend, not for his sake or Roxanne's, but for the sake of all society.

Chapter Five- Of Delusions and Dalliances

I was always taken aback at how quickly the scenery changed when going into Southside Haven. It was almost instantaneous. The tree-lined sidewalks would change to be filled with all sorts of litter. The beautiful architecture of the Upper North changing for the neo-classical, broken, and decrepit styling of the older buildings. The reputable businesses changing for the drug dealers and whorehouses that bewitched many men. It was a whole new world only a few blocks separate. I drove through a majority of the slums until I reached a large building with a half lit sign that read, *Backdoor Haven.*

The outside of the building was decaying, many bricks had fallen from the wall letting gaps of light escape from inside. The windows were all boarded up and there was a door with a large iron grate open beside it. On the sign, there was a large silhouette of a naked girl surround by neon lights. As I got out of my vehicle I nervously approached the establishment, knowing its reputation. When I entered the building my ears were assaulted with EDM repetitiously pounding out of loud speakers all around. Lights were flashing in no particular order and there was a distinct smell of something rotten emanating from every corner of the place.

As I looked around I noticed a few Loveless performing on stage in extremely skimpy lingerie. There were a few men around the establishment, none of which I could identify, but a few bore the marks of a declassified Loveless. The scorch of wings once there. When any Resonance breaks a major law they would be taken into court and their wings would be removed. No one understood how it was done but it looked as though they were burned off.

I made my way through a crowd of 20-year-olds towards the bar. The bartender looked at me and shouted, "whatcha' lookin' for?" The music was loud and my first attempt to speak was met with a very confused look. So I tried again, this time, raising my voice even louder, "I'm looking for Vixen, is she in the stronghold?"

That time she heard and she moved to the back of the bar and grabbed a small pinprick key. After she gave it to me, she nodded and pointed to the storage closet. I had been to the stronghold once before on an assignment. It was a glorious experience and I was excited to see if anything had changed. The back room consisted of many unopened boxes of liquor, a pole that looked like it was bent, and a small hole in the back wall. I put the key inside and was surprised when it was sucked into the key hole. The last time I had been here it was just a keypad but the key seemed to be better security. It was then that I heard the familiar hiss and click of the door opening. I stepped towards the slight crack in the wall and pushed it inwards revealing a long marble passageway leading down. The entire way lit by florescent bulbs built into the marble.

The passageway went down about two stories before I reached a set of metal doors. At that point I took off my shirt and corset, letting my wings fly free. A sensor recognized the extra appendages and opened the metal doors revealing a small elevator. I took the few steps in and waited till it started moving downward. The elevator played some of the music produced by the Loveless, music that was known for its immense beauty and entrancing style. The notes dancing around the elevator, cavorting into my mind putting me into a sort of trance as I waited for the elevator to stop moving.

Finally, a slight ding alerted me to the fact that I was at the stronghold's main floor. The doors opened and I was bombarded with the sights and sounds of the bustling stronghold. It was far busier than I had ever seen before. There were a couple hundred Loveless, Hopeless, and Faithless moving in all directions. Trees and flowers seemed to be growing straight out of the onyx colored flooring in rows down the entirety of the room. The room itself was ten stories high and had a multitude of windows cascading down the face of the walls. In between the windows were numerous statues of angelic beings and famous Hopeless and Faithless who had done amazing feats in their ministries.

I stood gawking at the magnificent structures and remembered that this was one of the smallest strongholds in the world. It was a small city and it was a Loveless centric stronghold. I had been to a few of the strongholds but I really disliked seeing the state of the Resonance society. After my first few missions as a Loveless, I had stopped using the strongholds only visiting to get the next mission.

Suddenly I was pulled back into reality by arms being thrown around my neck. I startled and pulled back from the assault. I looked at the feminine figure in front of me and smiled. She was a couple of inches shorter than me. Long flowing black hair going everywhere as she took a step back. Majestically silver eyes blinking as she took me in.

"Hey Vixen… long time, no see." I said as I continued admiring the stronghold.

She frowned at me trying to look mad but failing to do so, "Where have you been?"

"Working, I have a case. It was Gabe's direct order."

"You live in town right?"

"yes, but... I wanted to live on my own. Separate from the community until I completed this mission. To be honest I also wondered if you were going to be mad at me for leaving you behind when I joined the Loveless."

Her frown softened and she began to smile again. She sighed and then said in playful banter, "I could never be mad at you."

"Good, because I would like you to do something for me. It's important to my case. Though, I really disapprove of you doing it." I shifted my gaze so that I wasn't looking her directly in her eyes. The whole time I could feel her eyes drilling into me as I awaited her response.

"Alright, anything for you, just not out here. I'm not sure everyone here is trustworthy anymore."

She took my hand and led me down the large entranceway turning a couple of feet from the end of the room and leading me into a small passageway. It was lined with many doors of varying colors with nameplates emblazoned at eye level. She took me to one about halfway down the hallway. The name on the door was Mary. She opened the door and we went into a living area about the size of a three-bedroom apartment. Leather couches were positioned at one end of the room towards a fireplace on the other end. A large, super-realistic painting of a Japanese style rice field hung on the wall between the two. We made our way over to the couches and sat down facing each other. She wiped the hair off her face and waited for me to continue my explanation of need.

"So, I need your expertise in men. Controlling one for instance. Would you be willing to entrance a man to yourself?"

She shifted in her seat and sat up straight. Her face suddenly turning extremely serious, "Depends, why?"

"I have a couple I know should be together, my marks, but there is another man who is dating her right now. She is dating him just to make my male mark jealous. I need you to break them up by pulling her boyfriend to yourself. You are the only one I know who has done that before."

She smiled gently at me, took my hands in hers, and said, "Of course. I still owe you for sticking with me when I almost fell away." I noticed tears welling up in her eyes, "Just tell me who he is and I will help." I didn't want to force her to help me especially because she had once dealt with falling in love with humans.

We sat and talked specifics for the next couple of hours. Many topics came up including my love life, which was nil, to a Loveless she had been romancing and hoping to have a child with. I was happy that she was driven, like me, and wanted to take care of the child properly. She also told me about the oddities she had been seeing around the stronghold.

Over the last couple of weeks, she had noticed trees dying, when they never had before, and darkness coming from some of the most well-lit areas of the building. At first, she thought her mind had been playing tricks on her but she was able to get close to the darkness once and had heard voices coming from within.

She looked around her apartment complex and picked up a photo that was on a table to the left of the sitting area. She looked at it for a while before returning to the seat and giving it to me to look at. The photo showed a hallway with two creatures standing close to each other.

Both of them were black men with scorches on their back. They were once Resonance but they had lost their wings. However, there was smoke coming from the two holes where the wings used to be. Flowing down their backs reaching just above the tailbone. The smoke formed a wing like shape replacing the missing parts. They were dissenters, the Resonance who chose to follow the First Fallen.

Both men wore coats with a red symbol on them that I couldn't make out. They were in near darkness as they talked to each other. I looked at Vixen with a puzzled look on my face and she said, "It's what you think it is. They are Fal..."

She was interrupted by a rap at the door. There was a jump shared between us but she recovered quickly and made her way to the door. She looked through the peephole, then opened the door to reveal a male Loveless awaiting entrance. She embraced him and asked him to join the conversation. He was well built, about the same height as me and had some ruggedly handsome features. He sat down on the other couch and faced us.

"Core, this is Jafron. He is my...love." She took her time saying love as if deciding if she truly felt that way about him. He smiled and nodded politely. "I forgot that he was going to drop by tonight. Luckily he did, now you two can meet. Jafron meet my brother, Cornelius."

"It's nice to meet you Core, she has told me a lot about you. You both had the same mother Loveless?" He spoke in soft drilling waves, a deepness about his voice that didn't match his skinny stature. His voice oddly soothing.

"Our mother, Mary, gave birth to us at the same time. One of a few twins ever born to a Loveless. We still don't know who our father is." I was surprised how much information I was willing to give up to this man I had just met. I had to assume that he might be someone who could persuade people and make them like him. He seemed trustworthy enough and Vixen seemed to trust him, but I still didn't want to be too forthcoming with him, "But that's enough about me, tell me a bit about yourself. Where does the name Jafron come from? It's not very common."

"My full name is Joaniferus Ambitral Fallow Rotham Omerion Nixus. So to keep it simple, I call myself Jafron. The one who named me wasn't too kind."

"That name almost sound Latin, are you from this stronghold originally?" I was glad to have the power back on my side of the court. I intended to find out as much about this new suitor in my sisters' life. Though I also realized it was already getting late.

"No. They are made up names given to me by some lady who found me on the street." He shuddered as if shaking off a bad memory. "I have come to accept it as part of my past, though. Why are you here?"

Out of nowhere Vixen piped up with her feminine voice cutting off my own, "He has asked me to break up a human couple. Of which, I am most definitely going to do!" She had a forceful tone to her voice. As if trying to act tougher than she was. It was amusing and I noticed Jafron with a small smile on his face.

"Do as you must. I should probably go, I just wanted to see you before the next shift takes place." He got up and embraced Vixen again before leaving the room. I also got up to leave knowing I would need some sleep before the next day. Vixen decided that she would walk me outside and we talked a bit more about Jafron and about the mission. As I exited the building I turned and hugged Vixen one last time. "I missed you." I whispered into her ear.

She stood there contemplating her next action and then she lunged forward and planted a kiss on my cheek, "I missed you too," she had said it so softly I had almost missed it. She smiled again and I turned to get into my car. She tapped me on the shoulder and I spun around to look at her, "please don't fail this couple." she said with tears in her eyes.

As I drove home I thought about all the occurrences at the Stronghold and the new relationship that Vixen was in. I had an overwhelming sense that something bad was going to happen. This was forgotten about as soon as I got back home and looked at the clock. Half past eleven. The time hit me like a brick to the face and my body started to shut down. I sauntered into the bedroom and without getting undressed I flopped on the bed and shifted peacefully into my other reality.

The difference in my dream world was striking seeing as the mysterious girl was sitting right beside me at the beginning of the dream. Her face was defined better now with a mouth that was just the right distance away from the cute nose that I had come to accept. Her mouth had formed a half smile as if to say, "You know me. But who am I?"

Her lips were soft almost blending into the pale whiteness of the rest of her face. She opened her mouth but nothing came out. She just sat there contented. Then, suddenly, she stood up, mouth agape, looking kind of shocked as if something incredibly horrific were behind me. The lack of eyes on her face confusing the emotion she was trying to display. She took a few deep breaths with her mouth wide open and I waited for something, anything to come out of the perfectly formed lips. The words didn't come from her mouth though. They radiated out of the ceiling and the walls bouncing off of every object and consuming the reality around me. Those four letters that would not leave my mind. "STOP."

I woke up early sweat staining my sheets for the umpteenth night in a row. These dreams were steadily becoming more like nightmares. Haunting me and waking me up in the middle of the night. The worst part was knowing that the girl of my dreams was someone I knew. A face I recognized, but couldn't place. Her features seemed so familiar, but yet so outstandingly different because of her immense beauty, I just didn't know. The long flowing gown she wore didn't help matters either because it hid her body from me so I couldn't tell those features. I knew, slowly, over time, it would be revealed to me but why? What reason could I have for these dreams?

I got up quickly the next morning and changed out of the clothes I had slept in. They were quite disgusting so I threw them in the washer. Today was the day I was going to "meet" Steve. I took a deep breath and began transforming my face. Changing my features once again to hide my personality. I was already feeling the drain on my energy but I know that it would be refilled as soon as I went outside. I knew I needed to hide myself, at least for now.

The odds were quite low that he would recognize me but there was still that chance. So I wore something quite unexpected, a shirt with a Bible verse on it, and blue jeans with no hat, my snow white hair showing through. I changed my face giving myself less plump lips, brown eyes instead of the crystal blue they normally were and I made my nose noticeably fatter. When I looked in the mirror I noticed that I almost looked like Ronald Regan if he had lost a hundred pounds. After a few minutes, I was out the door and on my way to Starbucks

My plan for the day was simple. Find Steve, sit down across from him and just chat. I had to tell him about Bobby's cheating on Roxanne. I would tell him, he would call Roxy, find out I was right and then he would go to comfort her. It was simple. I just needed to explain how I knew. I understood that I looked like a football player, so it would be logical that I was a friend of Bobby's which is how I would know about his cheating. My only hope was that Vixen had already completed her mission. Which I was sure she would have. I let a quick prayer go as I pulled into the Starbucks.

I found him sitting alone at a table with his newspaper looking quite somnolent. I sat down across from him and he didn't even look up. I could tell he was depressed about where his life was at. To break the tension, I started to talk, "Hey man, I'm not sure if you remember me, from the diner. I was sitting behind you. My name is Cornelius... do you think we can talk?"

He looked up and nodded, a frown firmly planted on his face. His melancholy mood clearly apparent through his dress. His hair was matted; his eyes were dull with a hint of sadness reflecting the inner workings of his soul. He was extremely downtrodden and probably didn't want to talk to a complete stranger. I opened my mouth to start telling him all I knew when he shifted in his seat and started speaking. I couldn't make out any words since he mumbled, but it seemed to be about Bobby and Roxanne. Most of the words were too low and jumbled during his tirade that I couldn't hear them but the things I did hear gave me hope for him.

"Why can't she be with me?"

"She is everything to me."

"I don't like the fact that she's with him."

"I'm sorry I don't normally spill my guts like this but, Roxanne man, she's everything."

As he was ranting I heard the door open and saw Roxanne rush in with her face contorted in sadness. A look reminiscent of the funeral. It was a distraught look that was indicative of a breakup. Tears running down her face, mascara broken by the streams of salt and water. She ran up to Steve, threw her arms around him and cried, "Bobby broke up with me!"

I initially freaked about Roxanne learning about but me, but I couldn't help but see the quick flutter of a smirk cross Steve's face. Psychologists called it a micro expression. A brief but exponential emotion that shows how a person truly feels. Something almost impossible to see because of how fast it crosses the person's face. They were hard to detect but with training, you can notice them. This was a skill the Loveless had to learn in the early days of training because it would tell us the truth about a person's emotions far faster than just listening to what people would say. You could never trust a human to tell the truth about love. Mostly because they don't know what love is themselves. The only thing you can trust is their face and the tiniest of movements that implicate what they truly feel.

She sat there talking with Steve as I listened in across the table. I don't think she realized I was there until five minutes into the conversation. She finally looked across the table and said in a condescending tone, "Steve, who is your friend?" I could tell she didn't think much about my appearance which made sense since I was going for the bottom end of average for the look of my face.

Steve sat there for a few seconds before he said anything then just said, "This man is Cornelius, I met him at the diner the other day, we had a small conversation about the girls we like!" With that, he shot me a wink and I knew this was the girl he had been alluding to. Or at least, I would have if that wasn't already prior knowledge.

"Nice to meet you, umm. Sorry, I seem to have forgotten what Steve said your name was?"

"Roxanne, Roxy for short. It's nice to meet you, Cornelius."

My plan again was ruined by unforeseen circumstances. Though, it wasn't really ruined since he knew about Bobby breaking up with her and he was there to comfort her. Everything worked out, just not in the way I thought it would. She kept talking to Steve acting as if I wasn't there so I just amused myself by thinking about how odd the coincidence of Roxy coming in was.

The best part was that I knew for sure how much he wanted to love her. To make her his own. This was good but there were still a lot of steps to get through before they would begin dating and admitting their love for each other. I wished I had gotten a drink to occupy myself with. After she finished her story about Bobby she included me in the conversation. We all chatted together for an hour about a few odds and ends, like how the government should ban addicting drinks such as Starbucks. There was some laughter but mostly the conversation was morose. Though I thought it amusing that every so often either Roxanne or Steve would shoot me a glance as if to say "we need your input now"

Finally, Roxanne left to go home hoping to drown her sorrows in Hagen-daws and movies. Steve got up to leave and asked if she would like some company. She accepted and Steve told her to go to the car and he would follow. As soon as she left Steve said, "She does that every time a guy leaves her. I don't know why she comes to me but she always does. It kind of depresses me because she always seems to leave from my arms into the arms of someone else!"

I looked at him, locking my eyes with his, showing my disbelief and asked the question that was on my mind since we had first talked, "why do you think you aren't good enough for her. She obviously likes you, which is why she runs into your arms!" He just looked at me blankly. A confused puzzled look on his face. His furrowed eyebrows approaching the tops of his cheeks with increasing ferocity. After a few awkward seconds, he replied, "What would you know about it?"

I got up and took my jacket and said, "I have been around the bush enough times to know." I winked at him and left. I drove off smiling to myself at how well everything had worked out for me. The days were tiring and I had been working a lot so I decided to treat myself to a meal at the diner. Once that thought crossed my mind I got excited about the delicious food I was about to partake in.

I entered to be met with the same bubbly smile that always met me and I said, "hey Janet, what's the special today?" she led me to my seat and pulled her notepad out of the small pocket on her outfit. The checkered pattern ruffling under her movement. Almost mesmerizing in its patterns.

She looked over the pad a few times then she read, "The special today is chicken penne over rice. The Chef is trying to get fancy, "she said with a smile and a chortle, "What can I get you to drink?" she looked at me and I couldn't help but notice her natural beauty again. Very well formed for a human. Her face rounded off perfectly and her lips flowing into her other features perfectly. They were separated slightly as she smiled.

"I'll get a root beer and be a dear, get me a special. Thanks." She bounced off and I thought about my dream. The more I thought about it I realized Janet's nose was similar to my dream girl's nose. Though there was a lot of differences. The paleness of the dream girls face, the height of the dream girl, her colourless lips, and the shape of her face was different. I found myself disappointed. Thinking about Janet as my dream girl had given me a flutter of joy that confused me. I couldn't feel joy for a human being, like I cared for her in that way. That was just wrong.

Soon after Janet returned with my meal and I took another good long look at her. I passed her nose off as a coincidence and thanked her for her service. I started eating and fell in love with the succulent chicken within the sauce that was prepared for noodles, not for rice. Though the rice worked perfectly as a flavourful side dish. The perfect mix of sticky and loose.

After the small morsel of food, I went to my apartment to do more research preparing for another restless night. As I milled about the apartment I decided that I didn't want any haunting visions that night. The only way this would be possible would be to put me in a comatose state. Knocked out completely. This was easily done, just a little pill that would pull my subconscious from my body allowing my body to rest. Once in that state nothing but sound would pull me from the dream realm. Not movement, nor dreams would awaken me from that slumber. I would need to force myself awake in the morning so I set an alarm for myself.

I walked to my medicine cabinet and opened it up. There were a few aspirin tablets and a few other odd medicines in there that I kept for good measure. I reached in for the aspirin bottle and took hold of it but instead of pulling it out, I tipped it forward. All of a sudden, the whole cabinet swung out towards me and revealed a silver plated vault behind it. I laughed at my reflection glistened off of the chrome surface. I quickly changed my face back to its original form. Satisfied with my good looks again.

I typed into the keyboard 02 2:27 and the door clicked ripe for opening. Just inside were three items, the first was a small disk with wires falling down from it. When the wires touched flesh they would wind themselves around it and activate the small disk. A small blast of protoplasmic energy would then emanate from it. This was a strong weapon to knock anything back and blow a hole in anything it directly touched. I owned one just in case but I had never needed to use it.

The second item that was in there was a large book with the words "Veheili brem quayveheili" inscribed in a fluctuating effervescent font on the front. Which meant "the rules of order" in our own language, velei. Inside were the rules, all written in Velei with translations underneath in English, Mandarin, and German as some could not read our own language. These were the rules that we had to abide by but the main one was written on the inside cover, in the same font as the title, which stated, "Eeiem, breveh. Eeiam, tro emn. Buayeeivehl, helis." Which roughly translated to "Love, entirely. Hope, in trust. Have Faith, always." These rules were the essence of our societies and were meant to drive us to want to do the will of the Master. Though the Loveless seemed to be failing at loving entirely.

The third item was a bottle with six pills in it. I took out one of the turquoise pills and broke it in half. Watching as the pill slowly formed back into a full shape. The Loveless' technology was amazing. Self-replenishing medicine was one such advancement. Each pill was able to reform itself eight or nine times. I took the pill and sauntered to my bedroom. By the time I had made it back into the room and had my clothes off I was passing out. My eyes shuttered closed and I saw black, just black till eleven O'clock the next morning when I was woken by someone knocking on my door.

Chapter Six- Of Disreputable Events and Drawing Closer

I startled awake and blinked a few times. The sound of my alarm clock screaming into my ears. I slammed my hand down on it to quiet it. Then I heard the knock again. It resounded down the hallway breaking down my door and entering my mind. Nobody ever visited me unless it was another confused tourist. I didn't think any of my friends even knew where I lived. I made my way over to my closet and pulled on a large sweater and a good pair of sweats. The sweater was large enough to cover my wings. The soft cotton touching the pinions of light and making me uncomfortable. They were always a problem but right now I couldn't help but think they might give my image away. I quickly morphed my face into the Ronald Regan facade I had used the day before and opened the door. In front of me was a beautiful, broken woman so similar to Vixen but yet, so completely different.

"Vixen? Is that you?" It was all I could think to say, I had no idea why she would visit me. She just walked by me and took off her jacket and that's when I saw it. Two large, infected burn marks just off of her spine. The light streams still trying to protrude from the wound. Her wings had been broken off. Almost fully scorched. I also noticed a cut on her right side that was bleeding profusely. I quickly ran to get a first aid kit I had in my study for emergencies.

As I got to my study I heard her mumble something from the hallway. I looked around for the small wooden box that held some spare healing vials that I had collected from some of the Loveless strongholds. Vixen appeared in the door behind me just as I pulled the box down from its hiding spot.

"I'm worried," Vixen said with a hoarse voice. Her whole body was shaking from fear and pain. She stood in the doorway, her shoulders heaving with every subsequent flow of tears that came. She was broken down, hurt, and probably in a lot of pain.

"What are you worried about? What happened?" I asked as I rustled around in the kit looking for a small vial filled with a few of my tears. The healing vials would only work when mixed with a Resonance's tear.

Her voice was quiet when she spoke, it was almost like a whisper but it was clear enough that I could understand her, "I'm human now... thanks to you. I couldn't resist my urges once I had gotten Bobby to like me. He needed so much more than I could give. I messed up, I can't believe how stupid I was. He just wanted me to have sex with him... such a sick man but I wouldn't let him...." she paused for a few seconds as she blinked back the next wave of tears that seemed to shimmer in the florescent lighting. A mix of the lighted tear of the Loveless and the watery tear of the humans, "I wouldn't let him do it. I couldn't let him. He tried though and I..." Her face changed from sadness, to fear, to anger and back to sadness again as she slumped down further on the couch she had sat down on. She winced in pain as I applied a drop of the golden elixir on her wound. The flesh on both sides of the wound quivered and then pulled in towards each other. The cut completely closing in on itself.

I pulled her close to me and asked with a shake to my voice, "What did you do?" She looked up at me and just pointed to a large red blood spot on the other side of her dress just below her navel. It was almost completely dried. "You...you killed him." I just shook my head at the realization and said, "You can stay with me here. For now, is there any way that the police could track this back to you?" she shook her head but I couldn't tell if it was from sorrow or an answer to my question. I took her and led her into my bedroom and just asked one last question, "Did you lose your powers before or after you killed him?" She looked up at me and, in the most morose tone I had ever heard, said, "...before."

With Bobby death, it meant another funeral and another pain in Roxanne's life. If anything was going to happen between Steve and Roxanne it had to be before she found out about Thoron's death. I knew that Roxanne would be pulled down by her pain and Steve might lose any chance he ever had of dating her. I didn't know how I was going to get them together, but I had to make a plan. As I was moving around the apartment I had a vision of C'est L'amour. It was the perfect place. A romantic atmosphere, great food, and it would be like spite to the image of Bobby and her together. Steve would do far better than Bobby on a date there.

I left the house nearing noon after making sure that Vixen was going to be fine on her own. She assured me she would be fine and told me to go and do my job. She needed me to complete my mission now, her life as a Loveless would be meaningless unless I finished this. As I approached my car I noticed that the sky had started to darken. I looked up just in time to see two dots drawing all the light into themselves creating a dark sphere around me.

I quickly looked around for something to defend myself with but failed to find anything. I knew there wasn't enough light to use my powers so I just stood there waiting for the beasts to land. It took them less than two seconds to fly down and approach me. I stood my ground, holding my emotions in as I thought about what the Fallen were doing here.

"Ah, I'm glad you finally came out of hiding. We've been waiting to talk to you." The first guy, a man I recognized from the photo's I had looked through earlier, said with a higher voice than I expected for his stature. He was tall and far stronger than I was.

"I wasn't hiding. I was sleeping. What do you want?" I asked with as tough of a voice as I could muster.

"Well," The other Fallen said with a squeaky voice, "We need you to stop meddling with that couple you are hanging out with. If you think what happened to your sister is bad you don't know what we can do." He shrugged his shoulders as if he were trying to grow and be the same size as his friend.

"If you think you will dissuade me, you're wrong. I will succeed no matter what you throw at me. You should leave now before I destroy you." I pulled off my sweater knowing that no one could see me and flared my wings out to their full length. Their brightness cutting through the artificial darkness created by the Fallen.

They looked shaken and took flight using their own wings. One of them shouted back as he flew away, "you have no idea what's coming. Be warned, you should stop trying to get Steve and Roxanne together." Each word got further away as I put my sweater back on. Once my head came out of the fabric I was able to see clearly, the darkness was completely gone. I wondered what they meant by their threat. I would be able to handle whatever they threw at me. I was tough enough.

I got into my car and drove over to C'est L'amour, thinking about the Fallen the whole way. I got a reservation and left two hundred dollars to cover whatever costs they might have while there. Of course, this was a lot easier to a guy who was able to persuade anyone into doing anything he wanted. As soon as everything was in place I made my way over to Steve's house.

I pulled up just as he was leaving his house and I called out to him, "hey Steve, wait up man! I got something for you and Roxanne!" he turned to look at me with a questioning look on his face. When he saw me he smiled a bit and came over to my window. I held out the reservation slip to him and told him everything he needed to know. The more I talked the bigger his smile got and his eyes took on a vivacious tone to them.

"Thank you, I can't believe it. This will be so much fun thank you. I think she really needs it right now!" He seemed to be ecstatic about it. The surprise of my gift making him forget about the fact that I knew where he lived. He turned and left to go see how Roxanne was doing. When I arrived in front of her house I noticed a police car with its sirens still on. The police were standing on her doorstep asking her question. She had an inquisitive look on her face and was shaking her head no. I was surprised at how fast an investigation had begun. I parked a little bit away from the house and tried to listen but I couldn't hear anything over the sounds of nature and the sirens.

After about a half hour the police finally left and she disappeared inside her house. She reappearing in the picture window that took up half of the house. She had answered her phone and I saw her smile. I hoped that it was Steve asking her to the restaurant. I sat in my car watching the house for the rest of the day, noticing that a cop kept driving by the house every hour and a half. The vehicle seeming too dark to be driving around in the middle of the day. The inside of the vehicle pulling the light from the outside into the abyss inside the vehicle. It seemed impossible so I passed it off as my eyes playing tricks on me. Though I questioned if it was a Fallen.

Nearing seven O'clock she showed up in front of the picture window again, this time, in the same beautiful dress she had wore on her date with Bobby. I knew then, that she was waiting for Steve. I headed to C'est L'amour then so I could find a good place to watch the date from. I went in and got a seat at the bar until I knew where they were sitting. I would want to hear their conversation. After a few drinks, I heard the little bell on the front desk ring and there stood Steve in a nice suit. Roxanne looking better than she had in ages as she stood next to Steve. They took a seat on the far left of the restaurant.

I called one of the waitresses over who was in on the plan for the evening and asked her to seat me behind Steve and Roxanne. I had my trench coat on and I had shifted my face to look like an old man. I could hear everything perfectly. My waitress came by and asked if I wanted a drink and I ordered a water just to get her away from me so I could listen. At first, they talked about the fact the cops had begun a murder investigation on Bobby. The main suspect was a homeless man who lived in Southside Haven. He was sleeping when the body was dumped off but he had the murder weapon and all evidence seemed to point to him. Vixen had truly tried to cover her tracks.

Roxanne didn't seem sad at all that Bobby was dead. Her voice almost sounded joyous as she talked to Steve. Every so often her tone would drop when she would talk about the funeral, but for the most part, she was happy. The conversation droned on about the murder weapon, the man they thought had killed them, the investigation and many other little details.

I was worried that if they kept talking about this all night they wouldn't develop the relationship at all. I needed them to get closer, they needed to learn something about the other person but how could I do anything? I was relatively powerless to do anything about it. So I just waited. I couldn't expect them to develop a relationship in this atmosphere. My run in with the Fallen had caused me to try and push them together. Just as I was about to leave there was a slight silence, I heard someone shifting behind me and I could tell that one of them was nervous.

Roxanne sheepishly asked, "Steve, why is that we have never dated?" Roxanne's voice took on a somber tone as she spoke, "I've liked you since we were in junior high and we still haven't dated. Why not?" Roxanne seemed completely sincere and she spoke with a small lift in her voice as if she was trying to seduce Steve.

"I don't know. I never thought you liked me! Especially after the whole court issue and all the men you've dated. I don't compare to any of them. So I've been trying to stay away from dating you because I thought you resented me..." I peeked around the booth and saw that Steve had tears welling up in his eyes. He quickly rubbed his eyes to get rid of them.

"When it first happened I did resent you a little bit but I liked you, a lot, so I put it behind me because I knew there was nothing I could do about it. I really do like you Steve. I have just been waiting for you to make the first move. You know I would date you, right?" with that I peeked out again to see her place her hand on top of Steve's. "Let's continue being friends and who knows maybe soon we could actually date each other. I would love that but right now I need some time... I just had to deal with a friend dying but after some time maybe we could try dating?"

"Let's!" with that they both got up to go and pay. When they reached the counter they both had a look of shock on their faces. After a bit of discussion with the waitress at the door they left. Step two had gone quite well, despite the circumstances, but there was still a lot to do before step three could even be thought about. Sure they shared a sentimental moment saying that they both wanted to date the other person but they didn't really learn anything deep just what was out there already. They were now on the same page, so that made it easier.

This was a long process and I had to keep them together throughout the entire time. It was difficult but it was possible especially when they actually liked each other. For the moment, I had to keep them as friends until they knew everything about the other person.

Once in my travels, when I was in France I heard a man say something that caught my attention. He said, "Qui sait ce qui peut conduire à l'amour! Pas une, mais celui qui aime tous." Which means, "Who knows what may lead to love! No one, but the One who loves all." The purpose of this statement was to say that love could come at any time through any situation but in every situation, it was the Creator who knew what true love is.

This meant that I would have to keep a constant eye on their relationship in order to develop it into a true love. It didn't seem like the murder would affect their relationship too much, but it slowed the process a bit. I knew I still had to keep a close watch on it for the next few days. As I drove through the streets on the way home I started to consider Vixen's actions. Why would she kill Bobby? She didn't have any anger issues, she always had a cool head, and she had dealt with worse situations before. So what caused her to snap? I needed to find out more about his death. The Fallen seemed like they took credit for it but I didn't think they could control minds.

I pulled up to the apartment late in the night. I came in and saw Vixen stirring awake at the sound of my entrance. As soon as she was awake I sat down to talk to her, "Vix, what happened between you and Bobby?"

She blinked a few times registering what I had just asked in her half-awake state. She yawned and said, "Well, I met up with Bobby about an hour after you came to see me. He was just outside Baruke's. That bar in Eastbrook. So I invited him back into the bar to share a drink with me. Of course, as soon as he saw me he fell in love with me. So he immediately agreed. We went in and we had a few beers. Afterward, he invited me back to his house. So I went with him to seal the deal. We arrived at his house late in the evening, I think it was two or three in the morning, he was drunk so he started to make advances on me as if he wanted to... well... I'm sure you can figure it out. Anyways, after his first few attempts, I was already too angry at him because I didn't want that to happen because I would lose my powers so I hit him in the gut and he keeled over."

She paused for a few seconds to collect her thoughts. As she had been talking her voice had been getting louder and louder and with more force to it. She was angry about what happened and she probably had a right to be. She had lost her powers. She took a deep breath and continued her story

"I was so angry. Angrier than I had ever been," She said with a growl to her voice, "I wasn't myself and he just wouldn't stop no matter how much I tried to deter him. Then I got an idea that maybe a kiss would make him stop. I wasn't thinking straight. I knew my powers would leave as soon as I kissed him but it was all I could think of I needed to stop him... I kissed him and could feel a burning sensation where my wings were. That's when time stopped and the Angels took my wings. They were taken then..." Her voice cracked as her pain overcame her, "The kiss did nothing and he kept pushing in on me... I thought I was going to be raped...So I hit him in the face. His nose broke under the pressure...He stumbled back, I started to run away, then he tackled me. It was like something was controlling him and I couldn't do anything about my emotions either... His forcefulness didn't seem natural... I fell hard and I couldn't get him off of me. So I looked around for something I could use as a weapon to protect myself. I saw a cupboard open and a knife sitting there... so I reached for it and, well, I didn't stop 'til he stopped moving."

I couldn't say anything. I had never been in such a predicament. My sister had murdered someone and technically I was helping her. I was accessory to murder. Now, of course, I still had my powers and I could persuade them to let me go, but she couldn't. She had to fend for herself. She made the mistake of kissing him which was a sure-fire sign of love according to the Codex. In the human world, a kiss could mean anything. It could mean friendship, it could be a greeting, a kiss could even be used to betray people and it has been like that since the early days. However, to the Loveless a kiss was everything. To the Loveless, a kiss meant true love. It meant that you were sealing yourself to the significant other that you had kissed. It was the most official sign of a relationship.

"The court of the Loveless was brutal...I couldn't lie...I just told them what happened. They stripped me of all my powers...they had too. So, now I am human." She sat there dead to the world. No emotion that people had discovered could explain how she felt.

The Resonance court was a place that many had been called to in order to explain their actions. It wasn't always a bad thing to be called into court. Sometimes it was for a promotion but more often than not it was to be reprimanded. In the account that you were called in two Hopeless would come and carry you off, time unofficially stopping. No one could be certain where the court was, but one theory had that it was on the edge to the Creators home. Another theory was that it was on the edge of Tartarus. Still another theory thought that it was in another dimension. No one could be certain as you would blank out before you reached the court and would do the same when leaving. Only remembering what you said during the trial.

To think that Vixen had broken the rules shattered my logic process. She was always the one to be a stickler for the rules. She wasn't even one of the Loveless that stripped. She helped run Backdoor Haven but that was it. She was hardly one to go off and break the rules.

Everything seemed to be out of my control. I couldn't control how Steve and Roxanne progressed. Just help them to move closer. I couldn't control my sisters' actions as she fell away from the Resonance. I could do nothing to stop these events from occurring.

The only thing to do now would be to hide Vixen until she could get a place of her own. She now had to live a human life until she died, something that could only happen to a Resonance if they were killed by an outside source. She would have to find someone to spend the time with and work for a living. First, she had to stay out of jail. Hiding her in my place would increase her chances of staying out of jail. Plus, she was with me who had an upstanding record with the police less one little incident.

Back when the police had started getting better at tracking people down I was caught for a B&E. I didn't think about the alarm system and was caught when I tried putting flowers into my female marks place. I had snagged my coat trying to climb into the house and they had figured out that it was mine after a small investigation. I talked my way out of it but I wasn't able to bring that couple together. The man decided to push for a relationship too much while I was in jail and caused the girl to get fed up with him. The relationship ended with a black eye and a bruised ego.

I didn't like losing or failing, but every so often there was that one guy who would be so stupid that he would mess up a good relationship. Whether it was telling a girl a flaw in her beauty or staring at another girl as they were walking together the men always seemed to find a way to mess it up. The girl, however, had a bit of responsibility in them splitting because if she had reacted properly then they may have still been together.

I guess when it comes to relationships it does take two to tango. If a man messes up the girl could always be the one to blame and the same goes for the opposite. You never quite know who caused the issue or who reacted wrongly. In any case, there is always two sides to the story. A good relationship would take both sides and find a compromise in the middle. Even Steve and Roxanne had some things that could trash their relationship.

When Steve first put Roxanne's dad away she reacted wrongly. This caused Steve to act quite different from the way he had before. In the case of Steve messing up and Roxanne taking it badly, well, there was always the high school party story. To cut a long story short Steve accidentally drenched Roxanne with the punch. She overreacted and took it out on Steve by going the next day and asking out Melville Aesperns, the school nerd.

In both cases, it involved one of the two messing up and the other overreacting. That, however, was not something that I saw happening for them now that they had grown up. Steve seemed to have a good head about him and Roxanne was not one to overreact. They were the first couple I wasn't worried for. I still had to keep a close watch because even the smartest of people could make stupid mistakes.

A couple falling in love, police investigating a crime my sister had committed, and housing a criminal. Everything was a mess and I didn't know if anything would work out. One little mistake, one little flaw, and I could lose my job, the chance for love to flourish, and my sister all in one blow. It may take a while but I could do it still. I just needed to throw the police off the trail by adding in some extra evidence. In the case of Steve and Roxanne, I needed to set up a few more dates.

My sister said she could handle herself. I knew I had to start acting now or I would never win in any way. Starting this week, I was going to start attacking the system and bringing them to their knees. This week, I was going to bring Steve and Roxanne closer. This week started a new beginning and the end of the old. At least, I hoped it would be.

Chapter Seven- Of Danger and Disaster

It had been three nights since my sister had committed her crime and Steve and Roxanne had their talk. The investigation had been building evidence. Even though a lot of the evidence pointed towards the poor homeless man, there was more that pointed towards Vixen. The biggest clue being her blood at the scene of the crime. They had locked the homeless man up to be safe, but since there was reasonable doubt as to his guiltiness, he legally couldn't be charged.

The fact that the law was involved in my life troubled me. It was the last thing that I wanted to deal with. Though, I knew the facts. If the police didn't find the murderer within the first forty-eight hours, it was rare that they would ever catch the killer. Vixen wasn't a hard criminal though, she knew nothing and had made a lot of mistakes when she had killed him. The only thing she had going for her was her being a first-time offender and that it was mostly self-defence. The defence argument was immediately thrown out when she refused to stop stabbing him. It looked like a crime of passion. She had no remorse in the moment. If she was caught the trial would go badly for her.

With the paranoia, it seemed like the police were driving by my house more often. Each time I could swear they looked into my house, judging it as if they knew I was harbouring a criminal. It seemed as though every time I looked out my window a police car was driving by. This was mainly because I lived on Main Street in the middle of the business district. Cops were constantly checking to make sure the buildings weren't being robbed, that no drug deals were going down and that everything was calm. I still thought it seemed like they were judging me for my involvement and I couldn't bring myself to accept the truth.

I left my house early in the day around ten in the morning. I had to find out how the date had gone, I already knew, but I wanted to find out straight from the horse's mouth. I reached my car just as another police car passed by. He looked right into my eyes holding his stern glare. I couldn't break away from that look. It seemed like he was searching my soul as if trying to see where I stood in my heart. Finally, after what seemed like an eternity, he disappeared out of sight.

I breathed a sigh of relief. This feeling of guilt was excruciating, almost unbearable. It seemed like a shadow was beating down on me; making me feel as though I was being smothered. I had to overcome it, to push through and keep fighting for the love that had just started to blossom. I needed to cultivate it and to water it. Allow it to grow in the best way that it possibly could. Then it would eventually bloom into a beautiful flower that everyone would want to see and replicate.

I got into the car and drove over to Steve's place to see if he had left yet. When I got there I saw a squad car was parked behind his vehicle. Cops seemed to be everywhere I went. I hadn't spoken to Steve since I gave him the tickets to *C'est L'amour*. Between taking care of Vixen and waiting for Roxanne to get back to normal I didn't need to go out to help the couple.

I needed to ask him details about the murder and his relationship. So I waited for a bit and when the police finally left approached his house. When I reached the door I went through a quick checklist. Do I have my disguise on? Yes, I did, I made sure I did before I left. Is my plan still in action? I'm about to find out. Do I know what I am going to say? Hopefully.

I knocked on the door and listened to the sound vibrate throughout his house. After a few seconds, Steve answered the door. At first, he just looked at me, extremely haggard from having a lot of stress affecting him. His hair was a mess and he was wearing sweats and a dirty t-shirt. He looked downcast and beaten down. When he realized who I was he perked up slightly and invited me in.

He brought me to a nice couch that was situated in his living room. We sat down and both sighed with relief. It was a chance for us to relax and recuperate unbothered by our problems. I started off the conversation with a small topic starter, "So are the police getting any closer to solving the murder mystery?"

Steve let out a huff and said, "No. Apparently they found out about my relationship with Roxanne and they suspect I might be a potential suspect. Then there is that homeless man who had the murder weapon. They are counting us both as suspects, but they don't think it's us. They found some blond strands of hair and skin that were wedged under Bobby's fingernails."

The more I heard about the situation, the more it seemed like a self-defence argument was plausible. He attacked her and she protected herself. In the process she killed him. Sure she went overboard, but she had to protect herself. She was just guaranteeing he wouldn't hurt anyone again. In all reality, it was better that she killed him because it meant he couldn't deny it. It would be all hearsay and that meant that she had a better chance of making it through this if they ever caught her.

I looked at him and asked, "how are you and Roxanne doing? The last time I saw you I gave you those reservations to C'est L'amour." I knew I must have looked like I was pleading but I really wanted to know.

He gave me a dirty look then sat straight up, "We had a great night. It was amazing! I mean, she does want to go out with me but I feel like I don't know her well enough yet! All these years and I still don't know her." He had this half smile apparent on his face but it was hidden quickly overshadowed by a moroseness that had overcome his face. He shifted as if he was uncomfortable talking about Roxanne.

"Man, let me tell you a secret I have discovered over the last few years of dating. There are steps that can bring you together and things that will separate you guys. If she told you she likes you that is a good thing, it means she wants to date you," I paused for a second to let that sink in then continued, "The best thing for you and Roxanne would be to take it slow. Learn something new about her, be open and let her know something new about you. Then consider dating."

He thought for a second and then answered me in a very sarcastic tone, "well for all I know Roxanne might be a robot. It's not like I know everything about her or anything," he laughed, "No in all seriousness I completely agree with you," he lowered his voice after his hearty laugh and then just plainly stated, "I hope Roxanne and I will work out and I'm going to accept any help I can get."

We sat there and talked for over an hour and then he invited me for coffee since he was planning to go to Starbucks anyway. After a drink with Steve, I bid my leave and went to Roxanne's place to catch up with her. My plan seemed to be working ever so subtly but I needed to find out the other half of this story. I would have to find out if Roxanne was at the same place Steve was. As I left I saw Steve making his way towards the diner. He would eat and then head off to work, just as he did every day.

After the short twenty-minute drive to Roxanne's, I pulled up and saw that her car was there. I went up to the door and knocked. The door creaked under the slight pressure of my fist and I realized something was wrong. The door was cracked open, not just open like she had forgotten to close the door; there was a literal crack in the door. Right down the centre of the door, just enough that the door could easy be pulled off its hinges but not enough to be visible. I quickly pushed the door open and moved inside trying to be silent. Everything was a mess. Someone had ransacked her apartment throwing any object they could find in every direction. I looked around taking in the chaos around me. It was then that I heard a sound that chilled me to the core. A small whimper so softly uttered, coming from a room just down the hall.

    I followed the noise down the corridor slowly peering in every room to see if the small sound was coming from there. After looking into the kitchen, the living room, and a spare bedroom I reached the room where the sound emanated from. I saw a ball of clothes and limbs sprawled on the bed in front of me. Slowly rising and falling with a steady rhythm. The clothes were tattered but they still covered most of the body. The bed was a shattered mess around it adding to the disaster. Its whimper came in droves filling the small space with the sound of utter desperation. As I took it all in it dawned on me that I was looking at Roxanne.

    I slowly went across the room towards the broken soul in front of me. I slowly stretched out my hand to see if she was alright. As soon as my hand touched her she shot up. A terrified, dazed look taking up her once beautiful face. It was a look that pierced my heart and filled me with so much compassion. She was destroyed sitting in shambles. There were tears in her green eyes that were turned into a chaotic sea storm by the sadness that overcame her mind. She had dark streaks from where her make-up was running. I sat down beside her and wrapped my arm around her to console her. To show her that someone was there for her. I didn't know what to say. I couldn't think of anything that could help her so I stayed in silence until I thought about Steve. He needed to know what happened.

I asked her for Steve's number so I could call him. She slowly muttered out the numbers between sobs. I dialed and after five minutes Steve was standing in the doorway dumbfounded by the scene that surrounded him. The devastation that looked worse than if a tornado had gone through the house. Everything was displaced or broken.

"I was just about to leave for work. What happened here? Is... is she alright?" he was aiming the questions at me. He knew as well as I did that Roxanne was not in a place to be speaking. She was a mess, her clothes were ripped and there were scratches on her arms they didn't look to deep, but deep enough that she had to be in pain. Steve walked over and clasped her hand in his. Immediately she gave him a firm grip. She leaned into him and let her emotions out on his shoulder. Breaking down before the one man she could trust. Allowing herself to give up and surrender to her emotions. Her sobs turned into wails as Steve pulled her close. Trying his hardest to keep his composure as the love of his life broke down before him.

"I don't know if she's alright," I admitted as her wails started to subside, "I just came over to see how Roxanne was doing and when I got here the place was like this...She told me your number but I think she is in shock. She has been really quiet since I got here." I looked up at him hugging this broken shell of a strong woman. She released him from the hug but held tight to his hand as she continued to let her emotions break through her façade that she put up. She just sat there weeping, letting her tears fall off her face and roll onto his hand as they flowed out.

"She's a mess. I don't know who would do this! What would cause someone to want to put Roxy through this? Could it have been the police?" Roxanne stirred from her daze and shook her head to let us know that they weren't the culprit, "I want to do whatever it takes to cause more pain to them than what they did to Roxy. I will find them!" Steve sputtered as his cheeks turned red.

Steve was losing control. Anger was replacing sympathy. Rage replacing calmness. What was once compassion had turned into a cesspool of bitterness that needed to be quenched by revenge. I knew I had to calm Steve down. Talk some sense into him so that we could help Roxanne first. I asked Steve to come with me into the living area across the hall from her room.

"Steve, you have got to calm down," I said as soon as we were outside of Roxanne's earshot, "being angry isn't going to help Roxanne right now. We need to help her first, then we can think about revenge, or how to deal with this properly!" I made sure to put force behind my statements to make sure that he understood the severity of the situation.

He looked at me for a few seconds as if contemplating my words and then took a deep breath, "I know...I just, I need to be able to help her and I feel so helpless...Why would anyone do this to Roxanne?"

I could see that he was confused and that he was trying to return some semblance of reality back to the chaotic world. I put my hand on his shoulder and spoke softly, "The best thing for us to do right now would be to go and comfort her. When she finally calms down we can ask her what happened and who did this to her. Deal with the situation from there.

Right now, we need to get back into that room! First things first, calm down, call the police."

After a few seconds of awkward silence, he nodded and after we called the police we headed back into the room. Roxanne was sitting on the side of her bed. She was breathing heavily trying to hold back her tears but as Steve sat down beside her she broke into another deluge of tears. Steve returned to his position holding her hand.

"Roxanne, we need to get you somewhere safe. I want you to stay at my place until this situation clears up," Steve asserted as Roxanne looked on into a broken dresser that was off to the side of her bed. It was split down the middle with all of her clothes, burnt or torn, surrounding it. She nodded slightly after she shook herself out of her daze, "I want you to be safe. I care about you and I would be willing to take down every guy that did this to you!"

With that Roxanne looked up at him. The sea green of her eyes churning into a forest where her joy, hope, and innocence were hiding. She opened her mouth as if she was going to speak but then quickly closed it again. She nodded again and wiped the tears from her face. Trying to clean herself up a little bit so that she didn't look like a complete mess.

I motioned to Steve to tell him to try again. He took a deep breath and lifted her head so that she was looking right into his eyes, "Roxanne, I need to know who did this. Nobody, especially you, deserves to be treated this way!" With that he took her other hand in his and looked into eyes as he met her gaze, showing her that he cared.

Roxanne took a few attempts to speak coming out with only horse cracks or slight mumbles that were inaudible. She kept trying and finally was able to say, "I don't know who sent them...", she took another few breaths and then said, "It might have been Carolynne, Bobby's sister. She never liked me and she might have been the cause..."

Roxanne looked around the apartment taking in the maelstrom of pandemonium that had consumed what was once her house. She was bewildered but continued her story, breathing heavily, "There were a few guys, I don't know who, or what, they were. They came in and started to destroy everything. I tried to stop them but they attacked me, forcing themselves on me...they did...," With that, she grimaced in the pain of the memory. Her tear ducts refusing to give any more tears. She fought her emotions and kept explaining her pain, "They destroyed everything."

Steve looked at me in horror. I didn't know what to say. We sat in silence for a few minutes waiting for someone to break the tension that had built in the room with her story. What do you say to someone who had their life broken? Was there even a way to console a person like that?

All of a sudden Roxanne got up and cross the room to a pile of smouldering ashes and wood near her door. She reached down and rummaged through the pile looking for something. Maybe a shred of hope to hold onto. She looked back at Steve with a look that could have broken any man's heart.

"They destroyed everything... everything including..." her voice trailed off to a full stop and she turned for away from Steve. She cleared her throat and tried again, "even that origami love letter you sent me when we were young. I hoped, maybe, that it was safe but...it's gone. Burnt, like everything else..." Roxanne's shoulders slumped with her realization but then she changed the subject,' I know what one of them looked like. The one who...hurt me. He was tall, broad shoulders. He was surrounded by darkness so I couldn't see much but what I do remember is those eyes... So red...they looked like fire." She sat down beside Steve again and looked at him for something.

Steve didn't speak up so I said, "I think I've seen someone like that before. Or at least, I've heard about them. They are like a wives' tale. A group of people who were so consumed by evil that they became part of the darkness. Turning into evil themselves. They were called the Fallen. They also control beasts called the Skotos who were similar but less human. That's what it sounds like you described. I don't know if they are real though." I looked to Steve and he was staring at the empty place in front of him where I imagined a lamp had once sat.

Steve finally spoke up and said, "you kept that all this time? After all of our problems and all the crap we have been through." Roxanne nodded and Steve shook his head in disbelief, "Cornelius, why would the Fallen or the Skotos or whatever they are called, why would they attack Roxanne? What purpose would they have to hurt someone that has such a pure heart?" He asked each question with such determination that I knew he needed to have an answer.

"The Fallen try to stop anything pure from happening. If someone has pure faith, they will work hard to shake their belief. If someone has a pure heart, they will try to darken it by any means. Since Roxanne and you have such a pure relationship starting they are trying their hardest to break you too apart. At least, that would be my guess. I can't say anything for certain you know. I'm just guessing about the Fallen."

They both nodded and Roxanne looked at Steve with so much love in her eyes that it was staggering. Steve looked back at Roxanne and I realized that this traumatic experience had completed step two. What the

Fallen thought would destroy their relationship had caused them to grow closer to each other. I considered how to proceed from here and decided to ask about the love letter.

"What is this love letter that you were talking about?"

Roxanne looked at me and slowly said, "When Steve and I were young he did a huge thing for me... I didn't know how I felt about him but I woke up one morning to find an origami rose just outside my house. Inside was a note from him. It was a poem he had written for me. It wasn't even that good but it was so sweet. I put in my journal because I thought it was interesting."

Then Steve spoke up, "I still remember every word to that poem. It was ridiculous... I was so certain you didn't like me and I only wrote it so that you knew how I felt but...I knew back then and I still know now." With that, he sat up a bit and began reciting the poem,

"You take my heart, pound it into the ground,

You bury it deep, past the furthest hell.

You force me out to dig it up once more

It's been this way ever since I fell.

Fell in love though I don't know why,

Fell for you each and every time.

I don't know why I feel this way

But all you have to do is say "hey"

Look me in the eyes and tell me you don't care

And I'll just keep pushing this love affair.

I love you, and I always have,

But you fight me, beat me, tear my heart in half.

I get back up bruised and hurt

Just in time for you to shove my face in the dirt.

Broken and beaten I find shelter to hide

Within the inner sanctums of my mind.

In those moments, I forgive your hate,

I push away all my feelings, let them dissipate.

Then I return to you again ready for another bout,

Fully expecting you to break me all my days

I will keep trying until I reach eternity,

Because I love you. Always

Steve looked away as if embarrassed at what he had said. A feeling overcoming him that he hadn't felt in so long. "I was so hurt... For so long. Always thinking that I would never get you. Always expecting to fail. But I knew I cared for you. I knew you were everything to me. So I made you that note so that you knew how I felt. I have always adored you. I will always care. And I will protect you." He let out an exasperated sigh and gripped Roxanne's hand tighter. Sharing a look with her that I had only seen in a few people. They truly cared for each other. I knew what I had to do.

The next step would be an easy one considering that now would be a perfect time for them to go and visit Roxanne's parents. They were always good at solving problems and I knew Roxanne always loved an opportunity to go and visit them. If I played my cards right Steve and Roxanne would soon be official. Furthering their love that was so obviously shared between them.

I looked at a shattered picture on the ground and said, "I have an idea, why don't you guys get away. Go visit Roxanne's parents. Leave all of this behind and just escape to the middle of nowhere."

Steve looked at the photo and smiled, "I completely agree, if it is alright with you Roxanne I think a trip to see your mom is well deserved." With that, Roxanne nodded again. Steve looked at me for a second and then said, "Why don't we bring Cornelius along. He seems to be a big part of our lives right now. It might be a good chance to get to know him better. What do you think Roxanne?" Again Roxanne nodded and they both looked at me waiting for an answer.

"Of course, it would be my honor. I would love to get to know you guys more." The fact was I was going to follow them anyway, but they didn't know that. We decided to start making some semblance of the bedlam around us before we did anything. For the next few hours, we moved things into different piles trying to clean up, we talked with the police and planned for the trip to see Roxanne's mom. The whole time an air of melancholy surrounded the place. A residue left over from the Fallen. Pulling any high spirits that might be there down with it.

I left Roxanne's house late in the evening and headed back to my place to try and get some rest. The darkness around me seeming to pull all light into it. I pushed through the overwhelming blackness towards my home. Then, out of nowhere, the world around me lit up in blues and reds. I heard the familiar chirp of a police siren behind me and I thought to myself, "what could this be?" and pulled off to the side of the road awaiting whatever was to come. After a few seconds the cop, lights flashing, passed by me without even paying attention to me sweating from all the guilt that weighed down on my shoulders from the murder and all the secrets from Roxanne's predicament. I sighed in relief and proceeded on to my house.

When I finally arrived I was so tired I didn't think I was going to make it to the door. I made it inside and sauntered over to my bed feeling the drain of a whole day of disguising myself. All of my energy was sapped and I crashed onto my bed with a thud. Everything shut down at once and sleep overcame me. In my somnolent state of mind, I had forgotten to check on Vixen but I was sure she was fine.

As the dream came and went I started to realize something, the closer that the couple got, the closer I was to figuring out the identity of my mystery girl in my dream. Every appearance that came brought me one step closer to the identity of the women I had fallen for. This night she had long flowing blond hair. The hair detached from the rest of the time and moving with uncontrolled patterns. Beautiful but discordant. Soon I would know who she was. I enjoyed the mystery behind the dream but I wanted it to stop being a strain on my mind during the nights.

My plan was going perfectly and I knew sooner than later they would be dating. In three days we were all going to Roxanne's parents' house in scenic Kelowna, British Columbia. Steve would probably ask to date her then and that's when the true challenge begins.

Chapter Eight- Of Departing and Driving

Two days had passed since Roxanne had been assaulted. Steve and Roxanne dealt with the police once I had left and they ruled it a home invasion. They couldn't find any physical evidence of other people being in the house so they claimed that it was staged. The investigator thought that Steve and Roxanne wanted Carolynne arrested so they staged the event. It was infuriating and I concluded that the police couldn't do anything in this city. I would be surprised if they ever found Vixen. That was what had started the discussion on the thirteen-hour drive to Kelowna. We all were like lifelong friends who could talk about anything with each other. Already in the short friendship I had with them we had gone through a murder and an assault and I had watched the bud of a relationship form.

We had left at five in the afternoon after we had gotten all of our lives in order. I made sure Vixen would be alright alone for a week, Steve signed out of his work, and Roxanne made sure that her family would be willing to put us up. Then we all piled into my Town car to begin the trek eastward. The ride began with an extended story about the invasion. Every detail Roxanne could remember without completely breaking down.

"It is really hard to think back on that day. I was sleeping when I heard something outside my window. It was loud enough to wake me up so I looked out of the window to see what was there. In my grogginess, I thought it was just a dog, maybe a raccoon. I started going back to sleep when I heard something shatter in my house. I was so afraid, I couldn't move. I just listened to things breaking all around me. The more I heard, the more terrified I got."

She told the story with a draining tone to her voice as if just the memory of the event was enough to sap energy from her. She continued recounting the events, "Pages were being ripped, pictures being thrown on the floor. The next thing I knew, I heard wood cracking just outside my bedroom. And that's when they came into my room. When they saw me on my bed they made their way over to me. The big one knocked me off the bed and into my dresser. Then he hit me a few times across my face and scratched me with a sharp object, something that felt like glass. Once I couldn't move anymore he destroyed the rest of the room and then they all left. Right before you showed up."

She kept thanking me after that. The discussion ebbed and flowed through different things like where I was from, if I had a love interest, what religion I believed, and other conversation topics. All this time, they still learnt nothing about me. Every time she would thank me all I could think about is how I was a Loveless, a light monger, someone who hides in the shadows to escape being seen using light to claim my victories.

The more I thought about my profession, the more I realized how much easier it was now that I was in the open. I had openly broken the Codex and my personal code of conduct: Stay in the shadows. In all this I still hadn't lost my powers. I was still fine. Being that the shadows rule was often broken I didn't think I would lose my powers but I reached my hand to my back just to check to see if my wings were still there. I felt the familiar sting of my wings aching and I knew I was still normal. I affirmed that it was just a recommendation and not a rule. Just like The Process. You don't need to follow the Process but it helps.

Finally, a couple hours into the drive, when the conversation slowed and become dull I was given a few moments to think. Roxanne was the first to drop out of the conversation as the day waned into night. Then Steve fell asleep and as the night went on and I felt my eyes starting to droop as well. That's when I had a thought I couldn't ignore. One I had thought about so many times before. Why was love so hard to understand? It was created perfect, there was a perfect example, it's been described perfectly before and yet people still failed to understand it.

Love was easy enough to describe. I believe that when love is present everything around you falls away. You are left with the one you desire. Nothing else matters, but you don't actively seek it out. You wait patiently for it. You never hold it in contempt or look for something that is wrong with it. It is one of the strongest feelings within humanity. It is stronger than steel and more electrifying than lightning.

I thought about it for a while as everyone else slept. Thinking through the implications of Steve and Roxanne being the last couple who could fall into true love. Steve slept until I needed to rest so he got me to pull over. I was able to sleep for about an hour before we swerved off the road completely. I woke up and looked at Steve who was in a half-asleep state, "you need sleep man. I'm fine to drive the rest of the way. I've had enough rest." Steve looked at me for a few seconds before agreeing and switching seats again.

After driving for another hour we reached a small town on the outskirts of British Columbia. We had gone slower than expected and only reached Jasper. We stopped at a nice motel to get some rest. We didn't care, so we all got one room and flopped down on the beds at around midnight. The dream came and went with a ferociousness that sapped the energy I was gaining from sleep until I woke up far more tired than when I went to bed.

The next morning, I was the first one up. I went into the bathroom and took off my shirt and corset so my wings could fly free. They were just under five feet from tip to tip. The effervescent light filling the bathroom with an unnatural yellow glow. They touched each of the walls in the bathroom, caressing the pinions against the drywall. I flapped them once just to make sure they could still work after being cooped up for so long. They were sore but they still moved with ease. I loved the freedom of having my wings out so I flapped them a few more times moving them around in the small area. Then I felt one of them hit the mirror in front of me and it dissolved into a thousand pieces falling to the floor with a tinkling crash.

As the last piece hit the ground, a scream overcame the sound. Roxanne was shrieking in the bedroom. I slid my corset and shirt on and returned to the other room to see Roxanne curled up in the feeble position. Steve had already wrapped his arms around her and was looking at me for an answer to where the sound had come from. She sat there breathing heavily as Steve comforted her. Slowly, surely, she calmed down and relaxed into his arms. Her face curling into a smile as she realized she was safe. They were almost passing step three. I needed to slow the process a bit.

"What's up Roxanne? Why did you scream?" She looked up at me and at Steve as she finished figuring out her situation. She blinked twice and her eyes returned to normal. Her pupils dilating slowly as the colour returned. She shook her head as if trying to get her mind to sit back in the place it was supposed to be.

"I flashed back to...," she took a deep breath and stood up. "to the house. Like I said before, that was how they got in. They broke a window and that's what woke me up. It was just like this...I was so scared, I didn't move I just sat there. Now I'm here, running from my fear."

We were all silent again for a while with the sounds of the highway providing ambience. The vehicle was quiet until I said, "Sorry guys, I tripped myself and hit the glass pretty hard. I'm shocked that my hand's not cut or bruised. It shattered the glass. Sorry, Roxanne."

"It's ok Cornelius. I just need to get used to it. The feeling of always being afraid. The feeling that someone will always be attacking me." A tear rolled down her face as she came to the realization that her fear wouldn't just go away. She sat for a while looking at the floor before she spoke up again, "random tangent but is there anything else that we can call you? Cornelius is...well, it's a tough name."

I thought about it and replied, "I think you've shortened it before, but in any case, I prefer Core. It's a lot easier than Cornelius. Is it alright if I call you Roxy?" She looked at me, contemplating for a second before she nodded her head. She got up from her bed and began getting ready for the day wiping the tears from her face. We gathered everything together and we left.

There was still seven hours left to drive and Roxanne's mom was already expecting us. We knew we had to make it today. We left at around ten in the morning and were on the road. We stopped a few times to check out the sites and we traveled the whole way before we reached Kelowna at eight in the evening. The trip was meant to be relaxing and it was.

We drove around for a few minutes. We turned onto Leatherhead Road heading towards Roxanne's mom's house. We finally pulled up to a beautiful house on the outskirts of the city. It seemed almost serene with the mountains in the background. The sky dotted with a few clouds and the house sitting right in the middle of it. The light of the day was just turning to the deep blue of twilight with twinges of pink streaking through.

The twin pillars that held up the overhanging roof seemed almost like marble approaching the house. They gave off a slight shine as we got closer. Roxanne`s mom was obviously not lower middle class as most people were. They had money to their name. We pulled into the driveway slowly, looking at every detail of the mansion. We heard a door slam and saw a figure running towards us. Roxanne leapt out of the car and into her mother's arms. She was clearly outlined by the lights of the car. The other silhouette remained in the shadows though almost as if he didn't want to come out. I got out of the vehicle with Steve and we both went over to join Roxanne.

"Steve, Core, this is my mom Amanda and that man back there is my step-dad, Jake." She motioned towards Jake's general area and slowly he came out from the shade. His features were slightly darkened by the late night. He had a sinister look about him. A large smile crossed his face trying to combat the darkness around him.

"Nice to meet you sir and always good to see an old friend Mrs. Gersch." With that, Steve took Amanda's hand and lightly kissed it then went over and gave Jake a large hug. Jake finally came over and joined the rest of the group as we chatted about the trip and how everything went. That's when I noticed Jake looking at me.

"Nice to meet you both. I'm a good friend if you're wondering. We all thought it would be best to come to visit you guys. After the incident" I lowered my head almost like I was bowing to honour something that had been lost. In this case dignity, honour, strength, happiness, and the drive to keep on going in life. They stood there for a second before inviting us in to talk for a bit before we all headed off to bed for the night.

It was almost midnight when we finally hit the sheets. The discussion had run through many topics including the trip, how the three of us had met, the situation back home, and finally, how Amanda met Jake. It was a story of coincidence and "love" that started when Roxanne moved out of the house.

After Roxy was gone Amanda had started to buy a lot of unnecessary items to fill the void that Roxanne left. She spent extravagant amounts of money on televisions, sound systems, and a new car. Eventually, she started to run out of money. So Amanda went to an accountant and started to get financial help. Her accountant's name was Jake Froes. The more she spent the more often she needed to go see Jake. Money continued getting tighter and tighter and Jake and Amanda got to spend a lot of time together. They started to get to know each other and one thing led to another and they got married. It wasn't out because they loved each other rather Amanda was in it for the financial help and Jake was in it for the social status. It was quite sad.

Love was the main reason I needed to get Steve and Roxy together. They portrayed a love unhindered by material possessions. Too many times I had seen relationships forged through a love of the material. Two people who loved each other for the objects they had. One such incident was between Chris and Candice MacStevenson. He loved her for the video games she owned and she loved him for his car. There were other aspects of love in their relationship but the crux was those possessions. They eventually got married and had a child. When the child was about three everything fell apart.

During a particularly hard year for them a tornado formed in their city. There was no warning so, when it hit the house, they were not in a safe area. It destroyed Chris's car and took every item out of the house. While the spinning Maelstrom continued to ravage their house it loosened a piece of wood that fell on their child. The child, which was the only thing created by the 'pure love' aspect of their relationship, died.

The best part was that through this crucible, a true love had developed. They dealt with their pain in time and once the distractions were gone they realized how much they actually cared for each other. Their love grew until they died a few months later. They died holding hands at the bottom of Lake Eerie. Chris got distracted while driving and by the time he had realized his mistake they were slamming into the lake at a hundred and twenty kilometres per hour, killing them both instantly.

It seemed like the more that people fell in love with possessions, the more degraded love became. The more that happened, the more lost the world was. The world was slowly losing all hope of ever returning to a love which, once again, pressured this relationship to work. Steve and Roxanne would be an example to the world of how love is supposed to be. No longer would possessions gain any value other than just being a possession. No longer would a man fall in love with a girl because she could play Black Ops. No longer would people fill the hole in their soul with food. Love would conquer all.

Steve and Roxanne would also open the door to true religion. They would give way to a new view of philosophy and create new studies in science. Their love would be studied by everyone to find what was different about them. Love, when you thought about it, would be the perfect opening to most of what society had started to shut out.

My thoughts started to wander to different places and different times then. My disguise was starting to slip so I made my way to my room they had prepared for me. My eyes started to droop and my body was sagging. I let my sleep take control and just as my eyes closed I saw a beautiful girl with long, curled, blond hair and beautiful green eyes in front of me.

She appeared before I was asleep...She was there. However, I knew it couldn't be. There was no way she was real. The dream surrounded and consumed me. On the television screen, that had appeared a few nights earlier, there was a replay of the car crash that killed Chris and Candace. It caused me to start breaking down. In my sorrow, a soft hand touched my back. The lady of my dreams sat beside me and looked at me with compassion when she said, "it's ok."

This woman, this vision of beauty, cared for me. She loved me. Though it couldn't be real. I knew it wasn't real. My mind was playing tricks on me and making me think that there was someone out there that truly loved me. Haunted me, but loved me.

I just had to wait, eventually, these dreams would sort themselves out and I would know who this mysterious girl was but how long would I have to wait? How much longer did I have to put up with this indescribable horror? The thought that she was someone I didn't know scared me. I wouldn't be able to fix it, to run away, or make things better. All I could do would be to sit and wait.

I heard the alarm going off signalling the beginning of a new day. It had been another restless night. Sure, I had slept, but not as much as I needed. I felt drained, tired, and sore from trying to hide my true form for so long. I still had three more days before I could truly rest.

I slowly stumbled to my feet and walked across the makeshift room that was set up for me in the attic. I walked over to the window and opened it up to let air enter through the house. I locked the door and let my true form show. Curtains were drawn, door locked, and no way for anyone to find out so I thought I was safe. The light coming through the curtains hit my skin and slowly raised my energy levels.

I opened up my wings and took flight. It was a little shaky at first but after my wigs stopped cramping, I was able to stabilize myself and do a few laps around the room. As I was flying there was a knock on my door. I landed with a thud and frantically searched for my corset. I pulled it on and put a t-shirt over it and ran to the door.

Steve walked in with an angry look on his face, "What are you?" I was taken aback by his brashness. He couldn't have known. I had kept it a secret for so long he couldn't have known. No one could see into the room. He then opened his mouth again and continued on with his statement shaking his head as he talked, "You're a miracle man that's what you are. Roxanne is starting to be her old self again. She really did need to go and see her parents."

"I think a lot of that has to go to you, man." I said flipping the praise back to him, "You were the one who put all of this together. I think this is helping your relationship. You should let her meet your parents next!" I placed my hand on his shoulder and winked at him as if to reinforce my statement. He looked at me and tears filled his eyes.

"I.....couldn't. They died three years ago. Car crash," He took a moment to compose himself before he continued, "They died together. The last people I was able to truly love, before Roxanne." He turned to walk away and shrugged my hand off of his shoulder.

"I'm so sorry man; I guess the best thing for you to do then would be to ask her out. Right here man." He turned to look at me, his face flushed. There was a small twinkle in his eyes displaying his excitement at my suggestion.

"I was already thinking about that." He smiled again as he turned to walk away again. He finally closed the door and I let my disguise drop off again. I fell down on my bed shocked at the sudden change of plans. How could Steve's parents be dead? How could I have missed that? I read through their entire history and I missed the fact that Steve didn't have any people to take care of him. No one to love him anymore.

That would explain how he was able to start up an entire law firm from the ground up. I guess it was just one of those newspaper clippings that I skipped over. The Loveless obviously didn't consider that to be big enough news to have mentioned to me.

I slowly got the rest of my clothes on and got ready for the day. I changed my eye colour to a dull grey in order to show that I was tired. It was amusing that my features didn't show that naturally. I had to shift them to make them express my emotions. That was part of the reason I lost so much energy. Every aspect of my body had to be controlled separately.

I lost so much energy because I wasn't just masking my face. I was masking multiple features on my body. I gave less tone to my muscles and placed a little bulge where my abs used to be. I made myself shorter, changed my skin tone, and caused my hair to grow out. It made me realize just how perfect the creator had formed my body. He was very specific to make me look human but give me all of the qualities to make me better looking than them.

Today was the day Steve would ask Roxanne out. I could see it on his face. He knew it was time. Everything was going according to the process. Step four had flown by in a flash. Everything was going to plan.

Today was the perfect day. The sun was shining through rose coloured clouds creating a golden hue that shined through the mountains silhouetting them perfectly in the morning light. The day was beautiful, the time was perfect. Today would be the day that Steve would propose his love to Roxanne and ask her to date. That is, as long as Steve truly was ready.

Chapter Nine- Of Deception and Daedal Diatribes

It was four months ago when I began this escapade. Through all of the tough situations and the heartaches, through all of the troubles, Steve and Roxanne had come closer together. In that time, I had seen a shift in Steve's personality. He had gone from an uncertain, timid, and beaten down guy to a well-adjusted, time-tested man who would be a great husband one day. He was ready to begin dating Roxanne. I was tired though, ready to take a break. Everything had happened so quickly and I had been hiding my true form for so long that I was exhausted.

As much as I wanted to rely on my own strength; I know I couldn't. My strength came not from my own power or from my bravery but from the strength I was given as a Loveless. In all reality, any strength, in any situation, came from the Creator. His love and power would flow through us in the light and that would allow us to push on. It was love that gave us strength and love that caused us to act.

Humans were the same though they didn't realize it. They relied on love to get through life but without the loveless they would lose that sense of love. They would become lazy, obese, and all around apathetic. It was a sad but true fact to see in society, that love had disappeared and that people were starting to become less human.

I sat down and thought through my involvement with Steve and Roxanne for the day and then made my way downstairs. Today would be the day, it was beautiful outside, not a cloud in sight. The Mountaintops were shimmering with their melted snow peaks casting a haze into the distance. In the early morning light, everything in the house had a golden pink hue to it. It was everything I could have hoped for. A perfect day for

Steve and Roxanne to begin the rest of their lives together.

First things first, making sure Steve was going to do it. That he wasn't going to chicken out. I closed the door to my bedroom and turned around to head downstairs and was surprised to see Jake. His eyes peered past me as I stood shocked by his sudden appearance. He walked over to me and reached out his hand. His eyes glistening an odd color as the room around us started to shade over. Darkness surrounded the blue of his eyes slowly corrupting the pureness until his eyes had completely blacked over.

"I know you're a Loveless. Your disguise is pretty lacking today." As I stared into his eyes I realized: He was a Resonance. Though I knew he couldn't be a Loveless, considering he was living with a girl. A wave of fear washed over me as the darkness continued to swirl around us changing the beautiful day, that seemed like a dream, into a nightmare.

"You're a Resonance, correct?" I said slowly trying to figure out who he was, "but you couldn't be, you're married." He took a few steps towards me and grabbed my hand, a slight shock transferred between us. Slowly, he pulled my hand over his shoulder and placed it on his back. I felt the familiar feel of wings being hidden behind a corset. "How is this possible, you're married to Roxanne's mom?"

"I'm still a Resonance, per say, and I am married and 'love' my wife dearly," His voice was dripping with sarcasm, "You're asking me how it's possible?" He stared at me smirking as if he had just explained himself. He started chuckling as he continued talking, "I have removed the title of Loveless from my ledger. However, I have not lost my powers. It took me a while but I realized a flaw in the system."

He started to pace in front of me constantly shifting his features. His body went from tall to short, skinny to fat. He was basically just a blob of changing matter. He turned to me after finally sticking on a form that reminded me of Justin Bieber.

"Which of the laws has a way to get out of the Loveless without losing your powers?"

I looked at him quizzically searching his face, trying to find an answer. "I know that there is a flaw in the never reveal yourself law but what could allow you to get married?"

"You don't know the half of it. You Loveless are such idiots. There are some major loopholes in the law. Falling in love only applies to humans, changing form in front of a human is not actually a crime, and using your tears to heal someone isn't frowned upon either. You can heal others at any time. There are so many loopholes, but the one you need to know about is the Fallen Angel Curse"

At that moment, his eyes completed their transformation. There were no whites left. Only blackness with a fleck of red in the centre. His clothes started to flake off his body like ashes being blown in the wind. Slowly, his features began revealing himself. There were small incisions all down his chest with a circle surrounding the area where his heart was. A maze of lines and dots flowed out from the incision filled circle. The lights around us were flashing, some of them bursting with a loud pop. It was then that I noticed a slight aura around us. Obviously masking the noise and sights.

I took off my shirt and corset and took flight. The light under my wings giving me the ability to soar. All around him were flecks of his burnt clothing mingling into the darkness that now enveloped him. Through the shade, I could now see his perfectly formed abs and his fairly impressive muscles. He was well built, which caused me to wonder why he would portray a fat slob.

"Fallen angels are not even considered angels," I screamed at him, "they are demons. Satan's army. If you fell into that lot you are no longer a Resonance, you are a Dissenter. You're a Fallen! You didn't find a loophole; you found a way to become pure evil!" I flew over to his now fully revealed body and fashioned a sword out of the slowly diminishing light. The cold handle fitting perfectly in my hand. All of a sudden everything went black. I felt the sword losing its form quickly. I raised it in defense near my face. I could see the immediate area around me. About an inch or two in every direction but the rest of the world was like the bottom of an abyss. The darkness that surrounded this Fallen made the house seem so far away.

I heard a wingbeat behind me, floating into my aura of light. I ducked quickly just as a black shadow cut through the darkness. I tried to raise my sword to protect myself but couldn't find his weapon. I felt a knife slowly piercing my back, cutting up my spine. The gash pouring out my essence of life. I winced in pain as I tried to absorb the light to heal myself but the more I healed myself the more I couldn't see. I sacrificed my sword to continue healing but it wasn't enough. The darkness was too much. As the last aspect of light fled from the room I collapsed to the floor.

"You know, I was sent to slow you down, all this time I haven't been able to do anything, but now you walked right into my house. Now I am just going to have to kill you!" I heard a laugh I recognized so well from every dream I had dreamed in the last six months. That high pitched giggle from the girl of my dreams.

"Get out of my head!" I screamed to the heavens. I stood again forcing my body to fight against the pain. Then my eyes started to burn. A searing heat like someone had poured acid into them. I bellowed out in agony, squirming, dropping back to the ground. Suddenly I could see. The darkness around me dissipated and the world returned to normal.

"How does it feel being tortured?" I felt the cold steel cutting through my back again making me cry out in agony as my muscles cut apart, "to feel like there is no hope, to feel let down, broken, hurt!" again I felt the weapon slice deeply into my flesh. A new form of darkness clouded my vision, my body slipping into unconsciousness, "Now you'll know the pain I went through. The pain of losing all you love like I did when I was cast out of the Loveless!"

The last words echoed in my mind as I subsided to the pain. The agony was so intense. In my blacked out state, I dreamed of black birds and faceless women; I knew this was a trick being played on my mind by this Fallen. I couldn't do anything to break out of the eternal darkness I seemed to be trapped in. The black birds circling ahead cawed in a loud cacophony of sound. They then dived towards me prepared to strike my flesh with the full force of their downward dive. As the birds touched my skin a bright light burst through my eyes and as I blinked and cleared away the blurriness, I saw a forest.

I blinked a few more times as I regained consciousness, gaining more sight with each flutter of my eyes. I saw leaves slowly falling around me. As the light was slowly diminishing around me I realized it was sunset, I had just woken up though, how could it be night already? I must have been out for quite some time.

"Ah, I see you're awake. You've been out for, oh, about eight hours now! I thought I might have killed you." I looked around for the source of the voice that was so disturbing. The was a dark, clawing sound that rested at the back of his voice as if another creature was trying to speak through him. It sounded like a nightmare yet somehow I recognized it, "are you going to say something?"

"Where are you? Show yourself!" I tried to move but as soon as I shifted my body I felt an unearthly stabbing into my back. I screamed in torment as I saw a dark form coming towards me. The first thing I saw were those black holes in the middle of his face, the fiery red irises burning intensely!

As he approached I saw more and I recognized him as the Fallen that had attacked me earlier! His muscles were now clearly showing through a thinly veiled piece of cloth. There were large black tattered shreds of darkness adorning his back. His version of wings. His face had a shroud of darkness around it as if trying to hide his identity.

"Who are you, Fallen?" I spat out the last words as if they were a curse on my tongue, the pain I had felt before was stabbing into me yet again. I winced as I screamed out in rage, "Tell me coward, who you are?"

"You pathetic Loveless, don't you already know. I've been fighting you since this started. I was that guy who dated Roxanne, that 'dead' boy, and now Amanda's love interest," with that he changed his form. His wings becoming light, his clothes being bathed in a phosphoresce essence. He looked like a Loveless. That's when I recognized him. Vixen's boyfriend, Jafron. The entire time, all of the darkness I had seen, it was him, "I am the one that has been fighting you from the start," He continued, his voice becoming more sinister with every word he snarled, "I am the one who will not let this love continue! You pathetic Loveless, you will never be strong enough to fight me!" He was walking around me touching his cold steel to my arm. He was toying with me and I was too weak to do anything about it. In the waning twilight, there wasn't even enough light to heal me.

I tried standing, wincing as the pain coursed through my body. I looked around and noticed a huge pool of blood under me. "Why are you trying to ruin all the progress I have with this couple! Why are you trying to ruin love?" I screamed at him. His laughter enveloped my scream of rage and overtook it. Soon the only sound that I could hear was his laughter. It was maniacal, like a child who cannot stop laughing in the face of danger.

"Can't you see? I am trying to ruin love because it is the only thing keeping the Fallen from ruling." He stood over me and looked right where my heart was. He had this look of insanity on his face, "How easy it would be to kill you right now. You're weakened, beaten and bruised by my hand! You didn't even hit me. I could kill you in a second without even having a thought in my mind."

I saw a look in his eyes that I had seen only once before, the look I saw in Sarah's eyes after she had killed her husband. They had become stained with his death, a permanent scar on her soul that remained with her into death. It dawned on me then that a Fallen had possessed her, controlled her actions, and when he left, she was left with her actions. She killed Tom. This was unexpected and unparalleled. A Skotos was the cause of all the hardship in Steve and Roxanne's life. From the very beginning, the odds were against me, the darkness was fighting me. They were trying to gain their place in the world, trying to start a new breed of Nephilim. Those creatures of unrequited power that destroyed the world once before.

"You're a malicious and vile person. You're doing this all for power; do you realize that if there is no love left there is no reason for the creator to keep humans on the earth?" He looked at me with a look of confusion, contemplating the words that I had just spoken. I kept my stern glare and continued to try and persuade this Fallen to give me a fighting chance, "If the humans are gone who would you have power over? You wouldn't have any power, none at all. You would be alone, on a barren planet and you know that I'm telling the truth!"

"That's a stretch; you should know that we have been planning this out since the world was first created. Stop all love, control the Creator's only perfect creation then control the Creator himself! We've been scheming this since our forefathers were first forced out of heaven." I then saw a small black droplet fall from his face as he backed away from me. The black droplet hit the ground and a shriek emanated from the ground. Seemingly coming from nowhere.

The scream was bloodcurdling. It stretched the fathoms of imagination as it continued to grow louder with each passing second. It was louder than the clap after a flash of lighting, more frightening than a tornado, more powerful than a typhoon. It was a force of nature that stretched on for over a minute before it started to diminish. As suddenly as the scream erupted, the noise disappeared without any reason for it in the first place.

The look on his face was somewhere in between pain and anger. He slowly looked up with darkness welling up in his eyes, "He cast me out with no reason! He forced me to become like this, tattered, broken, defeated, it was all him! The Creator does not love; love is a farce!"

Another tear dropped from his face and yet another scream came from the nowhere. It took up the air and seemed to have a tangible effect on it. I felt it press down on my body, and I saw Jafron cringing in fear as well.

"My tears are not meant to be shed; I'm not allowed to cry. I must suffer without feeling bad for it. That scream is the unearthly scream of a thousand demons screaming for me to take my punishment like I should. A reminder of the pain I have to endure every day. You think you hurt right now, just imagine what I have to deal with. Every step I take reminds me of my failure before the Creator." Another tear fell and I expected another horrific scream; when it reached my ears I was prepared this time. It still felt like a force pressing down on me; trying to push me into the ground.

"It was your own choice to pick this way but if you free me I can try to get you reinstated into the Loveless. You seem genuine enough, but you need to free me." He took a step towards me and I saw more tears flowing from his eyes. With each step, another piece of flesh ripped off of him as if there was something physical holding him back, pulling him back from the decision he was trying to make.

"You must promise to take this curse off of me!" he screamed as he took each step. "Promise me!" After a few seconds, he was right beside me, he raised his sword and screamed in agony as he snapped the chain on my wrist in two. I hadn't realized that it was the cause of my pain until it fell to the ground. As he struck down he sliced deeply into my wrist as well. Pain exploded up my arm as I tore the piece of steel from my arms and I threw it to the ground.

"I promise," I said. I was finally free and I took flight as I turned back I saw Jafron being torn to shreds by the invisible force. I shed a tear that dropped to the ground and the forest was lit up. As the light spread out from my tear, I could see a few black forms attacking the Fallen with unfathomable weapons. With each strike Jafron sunk further down towards the ground. His strength obviously failing him. I quickly flew down to protect the man I said I would help.

As soon as I touched the ground the Skotos turned and looked at me. Jafron was behind them staring at me with a look of disbelief. He screamed out in rage, "What are you doing! I know you promised, but you can't help me! I'm done for. Please, just leave!" He shed another tear and the Skotos closest to him knocked him out with a swift hit to his temple. I formed a sword out of the light that had been provided by my tear.

I shifted my body weight to prepare for an attack. I raised my sword into a defensive stance and smiled as the Skotos stood there expecting me to make the first move. Finally, after getting fed up with the blank stares I struck. I moved fast but when I got close enough the Skotos just strafed to the side. He reached down and took a hold of my ankle, and bit deeply into my flesh. I screamed as I flipped my body over and stuck my sword into the flesh of the closest Skotos. It backed up and looked down at his body in disbelief as black tar flowed from his wound.

Then I looked again at the Skotos that had just bit my ankle. Flesh still hung from his mouth as it stood there pleased with itself. Then it moved over to his friend that I had just stabbed and let my flesh drop onto his wound and I saw the flesh form a new skin over top of the wound. The beast jumped to his feet and let out a scream that filled the forest. I flew up into the air and threw my sword at the ground where my tear was. As it hit the tear an explosion of light burst forth. Its force knocked each of the Skotos to the ground and bent the trees creating a perfectly circular arena to fight in. I shed another tear creating another light to see with. I felt my power waning and landed on the ground to catch my breath. The Skotos had almost recovered from the explosion. Looking even more grotesque than they had been before.

I had forced myself to get up and I looked east to where the sun was quickly receding. I needed the real light to heal myself but I knew it wasn't coming. I threw my sword at the demon that had bit my ankle and after a few flips, it pierced its skull with a deafening crack and an ear piercing scream. It slumped to the ground before dissipating into the air in a burst of ashes.

"Don't stand in our way!" The healed Skotos hissed at me as he jumped over the ash pile that was his friend. "We will win, one day." I fashioned another sword out of the light and hurled it in their direction as they disappeared in a puff of smoke. The Skotos were gone, for now. I looked over at the quivering piece of meat that had once been Jafron. I reached out and looked up as I saw the sun finally disappearing behind the mountains. As I passed my hand over his body I saw tendrils of light reaching out from my hand. They grasped onto him pulling him into an embrace.

"Why are you helping me? I tried killing you not ten minutes ago!" He managed to push out as his body convulsed from the light entering into his body. Slowly flecks of his skin shed off of his body disappearing into ash as he convulsed slowly his chest started to rise and fall in a steady rhythm. I kept the healing process going as I shed a tear onto a gash in his side that looked fatal. In a matter of seconds, it was back to normal. I was weak but I had promised to help him.

"I promised you and if you were dead I couldn't keep that promise," I whispered into his ear as he looked at me longingly. He reached his now almost healed arm out and touched my hand.

"You should let me die. I do not deserve this treatment. I tried to kill you... and in my rage I almost did..." A small tear exited the side of his eye a mixture of darkness and light and when it hit the ground a small plant grew. A red bud was on the top, a mixture of light and dark giving life to a plant. It was a rose. The darkness protruding from the thorns that punctured all those that tried to pick it up from the ground, the light forming the immense beauty of the red bud.

"How evil is a man who created life with his tear." I turned his head so he could see his creation beside him. He just stared in amazement as he lay there comatose. As the last flake of darkness left his body and I stood up and backed away from him.

His body started to shake with an unearthly shake that seemed to emanate from his heart. He opened his mouth and when I expected to hear a scream I was shocked when I heard a song. A beautiful bass voice came from the heart of his body as the darkness left him in the song.

"This life I've been living,

Is a shame to all who lived the same,

I'm sorry for those I've hurt,

I'm sorry for my curse,

But take my soul,

And break it free,

My heart is all for You,

All for You,"

It was beautiful and it was pure. The song bellowed deeply with beautiful dips and curves as he went from the deepest voice he had to a very high pitched voice and all with perfect precision. It was beautiful and it was true,

"From the deepest core of my heart,

To the final frontier of heaven,

I will shine my heart,

I will shine my light,

No one can tell me to back down,

No one can tell me to leave,

I am a one man show,

With a thousand friends helping me!"

Finally, the singing stopped and he stopped convulsing. We both lay there drifting into sleep on the forest ground weakened from the exchange. An empty mind was all that met me as I slept the night hours away. I woke up while it was still dark out. Only a slight glow was showing as the sun began to creep up the backs of the mountains.

Streaks of light shone through the oval of destruction that surrounded us. He got up slowly, his pure white wings shimmering behind him in the dawn light. Small specks of dust around him were illuminated with the rays of sunlight shining through the trees and I saw his silhouette outlined by the golden hue of the dust.

I clasped his hand and he pulled me close, "you have freed my soul and I will repay you by making sure that Steve and Roxanne make it. I will give them the 'fathers' blessing," He pulled his hand back and took a step back from me, "Thank you so much!"

"Just remember, this means you cannot continue with Amanda." I looked at his now pure blue eyes as he stood at attention tilting his head in confusion. "I know it is hard to understand but as a Loveless, we may not love ourselves. That is the one curse that we have, we can cause love but never experience it! Please, go and find Gabriel. You'll find him in one of the Loveless strongholds."

"I understand! I have that figured out. I am going to go missing," He moved his fingers in quotations as he said the word missing, "After my conversation with Steve I will say something that will seem crazy then I will disappear. I will try to keep tabs on you guys. Watch your back man the Fallen don't give up easily!" Then he turned and flew off. I took a few seconds and just sat down; I had never before experienced anything so invigorating. I took a few deep breaths and flew over to the edge of the forest. I was on the edge of a cliff overlooking some farm lands, it wasn't far from Kelowna but it was a fair distance.

I took flight and touched down just outside of Kelowna at just about ten in the morning. I walked through the streets and found my way to the place I would call home for the next day or so. As soon as I walked onto the property I saw a flash of clothes coming towards me. Roxanne jumped into my arms and I felt a tear or two hit my shoulder.

"Where have you been, Steve and I have been so worried." She took a few steps back and studied my face which was back to the fat face I had adopted as my persona. I looked around at the three faces and I mustered up my voice.

"Where is Jack? I need to know where he is." I said and then quickly added, "I'm sorry I've been gone so long, what did I miss around here?" The mention of Jack had brought more emotion to the already distraught faces I saw around me, "I'm guessing he's gone to"

"He came to talk to me this morning," Steve said as he took a breath to steady his nerves, "He told me flat-out, 'Steve go for Roxanne' then he turned and left and we haven't seen him since. That was early this morning that he had approached me" A sense of worry had replaced the sense of sadness that had washed over their faces. They all looked at me as if searching for the answer.

"I did see him as I walked into town this morning, sadly he didn't say anything. He just nodded and kept walking into the ditch and then into a farmer's field. He was so calm it was creepy. I just kept walking. Somebody kidnapped me while I was sleeping." Then Amanda ran into the house and I knew she was calling the police. She came out with the phone to her ear and she motioned for me to follow her into the house. As I passed by Steve I winked at him and I saw the same sparkle in his eye that I had seen a few evenings before when we had first arrived.

I entered into the house to be bombarded with questions from Amanda. Who are you, do you know who kidnapped you, where did they take you, are you injured, and a few other questions entered and left the air in the space of a minute as I came up with something to satisfy the police. The whole time I watched as Steve took hold of Roxanne's hand.

After a few minutes I was free and I slowly left the house to listen to the conversation between Steve and Roxanne. I wanted to hear the fruits of my labour, the final outcome of all my work over these last few months.

"Roxanne. We have known each other since we were kids, I have loved you since the first time we kissed on that dare back in grade school and I think I will always love you. I don't know why it has taken me this long to tell you. I want to date you so that we can be together forever. Will you be my girlfriend?" Steve said in a deep voice that was a little bit different for him.

"I don't know what to say. After all this time, you finally ask me out. I have been waiting and through this turmoil, I was reminded why I was waiting. I love you. You are always there for me and you always know what I need," she took Steve's other hand in hers, "I accept, I will be your girlfriend. On one condition that is!" Roxanne said with a little bit of a tease in her voice. Steve looked on with a dead stare, looking at her as she said, "You must promise that you will never leave me!"

"I accept your condition!" Steve leaned over and kissed Roxanne, her eyes fluttering in surprise. She slumped into the embrace as they passionately kissed for the first time as a couple. After a while, they released their kiss and looked longingly into each other's eyes before Steve noticed me out of the edge of his eye.

"How much did you see?" He asked me as he and Roxanne walked over hand in hand.

"Enough to know you guys are dating, congratulations!" I took hold of Steve's hand and whispered into his ear, "The first date as a couple is all on me, wherever you want to go, whenever, just find me." I leaned over to Roxanne then and whispered into her ear, "I know that you are surprised but trust me it's real. I want you guys to be happy. Please keep in contact with me."

They both nodded in agreement as I turned and entered into the house to be met with a hug from Amanda, "I'm so glad you're safe, I just hope you enjoy the rest of your stay with us here." She released her hug then went over to Roxanne and threw her arms around her and cried on her shoulder as she sputtered something about being happy for her and Steve.

I was worried that things had gone too far but now that they were together all I had to do was keep them together. It wasn't that it was hard so much as it was tedious. I had to look into every aspect of their relationship making sure that nothing was going to go wrong.

The hardest part would be getting them to fall in true love. I could do it of course but it was definitely a challenge in a different way, every day. I now had to account for secrets, denials, pain, hurt, and a whole bunch of other factors that could hurt the relationship that now existed between the two of them.

The four of us talked for the next two hours then the police showed up to question me about the disappearance of Jack and my kidnapping. We talked for a good four hours before they left and then Steve, Roxanne, and I all packed up to leave. We got on the road just after two and I started to get anxious about Vixen. For four days now she had been alone, who knew what could have happened to her.

As we were driving away I looked back and saw a flash of darkness outlined by the near setting sunset and I knew that Jafron was following us. I still had to worry about the two Skotos that had attacked me in the forest. I knew they were following as well. They had a mission to succeed at also. They were ruthless and I would have to send them back to hell before they would give up.

After a few hours, we reached Jasper and we stayed at the same motel that we had stayed at on the way up and surprisingly we got the very same room we had before. It was shocking and yet, in a way, serendipitous. We got in and I went into the bathroom and looked at the rigid and cracked mirror. The fragmented pieces seemed to reflect the feeling I had in my heart. They were broken, confused, angry and sporadic. I quickly ran my hand over the broken glass as I wept a tear that went down the drain giving a light that shone out brightly for a few second before disappearing into the sewers.

I left the room and lay down on the bed, exhausted after all the events of the past few days. I needed rest and as my eyes fluttered shut I thought, I might win this one! Then the dream came, realer than ever before.

Chapter Ten- Of Demons and Diminishing Dominance

It started just like any other dream. I woke up in the bed in what I accepted as my other reality. I looked around to see if I could see that now familiar sundress. Hear the now familiar sound of her laughter. However, she was nowhere to be seen. I sat up on the imaginary bed and looked around the room. She wasn't there but everything else was. Photos of us together were scattered on the wall. The bed was messy with pillows scattered around it.

Everything seemed so real. The rustle of the bed sheets against the comforter as I moved. The cold snap as my feet hit the floor. The fresh breeze of a window cracked open. The blinding light of the sun shining through curtains lighting the room with a hazy golden glow. I stood up hearing the familiar creak of my knees as they popped into place. My body acting as though I had woken up in real life. The slight pain disappearing as soon as it came.

It was too real. For everything I did in my dream, I felt in real life. I went to the kitchen and splashed water on my face. I felt it as each droplet of water hit my face in succession. I got a burst of energy as the cold water woke me up. However, I did not wake up from the dream, I only woke up within the dream. It was invigorating and yet it didn't settle the uneasiness that was creeping into my stomach.

I was confused and dazed. How could I feel energized and awake in a place formed by my subconscious? Then fingers grazed my back, tickling my wings as they went up my back. I spun around to be met with a kiss from the now gorgeous girl. Her plump red lips locked with mine in a kiss that sent shivers down my spine.

The feeling was intense. A thousand suns had lit inside my heart and I didn't want to put them out. I was in a complete state of shock and awe. I had never felt anything so pure, so strong, and so passionate. I had seen it so many times in the faces of those I have helped but never had I felt the overpowering joy of a kiss. It took my soul and shattered it into a thousand pieces just to repair it in a new way.

I felt weak-kneed and I slowly sank to the ground as she stood over me, her beauty making me feel worthless. I sat there for a few seconds weeping over the feeling I had just encountered. This was what the Loveless had been missing for so many years. This feeling of pure unadulterated happiness. It was non-existent in our society. Love was gone from the people who professed to know the most about it. I wanted more, I needed more.

The girl let out a little giggle then skipped away, her dress swishing behind her as she went. Then she stopped, swaying slightly. She turned towards me and shot me a glare that shook me. She ran forward and stopped right in front of my face. I felt her breath wafting towards me and I looked straight in her eyes. Her beauty overwhelming me.

That was when I knew I was still in a dream. Her pupils started to shift, creating silhouettes of objects, first a car, then a house. Soon her eyes were shifting through a myriad of objects like a bird and a human before colour started to seep in from her iris. The subtle blue tones shifting and forming greens and blues and reds throughout her eyes. Everything I saw astounded me.

I finally started to recognize what was being shown to me. I was watching the story of bringing Steve and Roxanne together. It went from our first meeting, to the murder of Bobby Thoron, to my fight with Jafron. Soon I realized we were into something that hadn't happened yet. I saw blue and red lights flashing in her eye, then a door closing and another one opening. After that, her eyes returned to normal.

She opened her mouth and softly whispered into my ear, "Some of what you have seen has already happened. Some of this has not yet happened, and some cannot yet be understood. Remember this! Love is not what you make of it but what you feel inside." She turned and left running outside the house and disappeared into a grove of trees just visible through the patio window.

After sitting in shock for a what seemed like hours, I made my way back to the bed. I fell asleep in the dream and reawoke in the real world. Disoriented, tired, and overwhelmed by the visions that were already fading from mind I sat up to prepare myself for the day. Quickly I got up and felt my feet touch carpet. I heard the creek of my knees and the unforgettable pain of long gone injuries. I knew that I had woken up in the real world when I saw the sleeping forms of Steve and Roxanne in the cot and bed beside me. I got up and went into the bathroom. I avoided eye contact with the broken form that was in the bathroom to avoid having my heart torn apart by sadness.

I couldn't understand why I was sad but I knew that it had to do with the kiss I had shared with the phantom in my mind. My jeans were tattered from the battle, my shirt filled with dust. I also knew hair was a mess but I didn't dare look myself in the eyes. It would have destroyed me. So, after quickly washing my face and reinvigorating myself with the warm water, I left to rest a few more minutes.

As I exited the bathroom I saw Roxanne stir awake. She looked around the still dark room and saw me. Silently she sat up and motioned for me to come over to her. As I walked, I noticed her smile at me in a very sweet and sincere way. I finally got to her cot and I sat down across from her on my bed.

"You, my friend, are amazing. I would kiss you but, my boyfriend is sleeping right there," she nodded in Steve's direction and giggled as she said boyfriend with a giddy schoolgirl voice, "I want to thank you for helping with everything. It's been rough for us for so many years and now that you're here everything is just... Well, I don't want to say easy, with my step dad leaving and the police investigating a murder that I was tied to. It has been simpler, though. To be honest I feel like you bring people together for a living!" with that she took hold of my hand and looked into my eyes. I almost expected to see her pupils start moulding and shifting as they had done in my sleep but they remained their same unyielding consistency.

"I live to love and to see love. So if I see a couple, like you and Steve, who obviously like each other, I try to help. It's more like a hobby than a job. Something I like to do in my spare time." I said as I stood up and started to make my bed. At that moment, Steve stirred awake and mumbled some kind of greeting to us and we all moaned out greetings back.

After a few minutes of waking up, and the worst motel coffee, we left. As we opened the doors to the car Roxy said, "Wait till you hear about the messed up dream I had. I can remember it so clearly." We checked out of the hotel early enough to be on the road by eight. We were driving for about a half an hour before anyone spoke. We were all tired and a little bit nervous about our lives back home.

Finally, Roxanne spoke up, "I had the dream again Steve, the one where I fall for you and you pick me up and we head off into the sunset. But, it was different tonight. You looked into my eyes and I saw your eyes changing. Then you just stood up and started to leave while saying something. It was about love being what you make of it or something like that. I didn't like it and I still don't know what to think of it."

The silence in the car was thick after Roxy had finished telling her story. I was thinking about how similar it was to my dream and Roxanne just didn't know what else to say. Steve seemed to be Roxanne's faceless woman and the similarities between them were too coincidental.

Steve turned a corner and spoke up. He was almost laughing as he said, "That's interesting because I had the same dream. With the exception of you being over me. That and when you got up you said, 'fear is only an inhibition, it can close your mind to all feelings of love but you can overcome it.' I don't even know what that means."

I was the next one to speak and it started out with a croaky voice, "I also had the same dream, the girl in my dream said something along the lines of one door opening and another door opening. I wonder if it all fits together." Roxanne immediately turned around and looked at me with a puzzled look. Her eyebrows were furrowed more than I thought was possible. In the rearview mirror, I could also see Steve sitting with a look of exasperation.

"It would make sense," Steve replied with his voice a little hesitant, "If you put all three together it says, 'fear is only an inhibition that can close your mind to all feelings of love. If one door closes another will open and love is what you make of it. In a way it kind of makes sense. It just says that we should make love our own. We shouldn't just conform to what other people think love is. That kind of love is broken and flawed. This love must be our own." Steve smiled as he finished his grand conclusion looking at Roxanne.

I knew what Steve and Roxanne didn't, that our dreams were connected, they had to be. Someone was now toying with us. I knew that the Fallen could possess a person's body, but I didn't think that they could implant ideas into a person's mind. So, how we all had basically the same dream was beyond me. It weighed on my mind the whole day as I went through explanations in my mind like mass hallucinations, coincidence, and a few other ideas but none of them seemed to fit just right.

The hardest part to explain was how I actually felt everything within my dream. The more thought about it the more I realized that there was no explanation. The floor in the motel was carpet, not wood or linoleum, so I couldn't have got cold feet from that. The sinks in the bathroom only poured out warm water, so I couldn`t have splashed cold water on me. None of it made any sense. It was impossible and yet it had happened.

We arrived at home close to two in the afternoon and after saying a quick goodbye I left to go to my house. As soon as I arrived Vixen came running out and threw her arms around me. She was crying in soft sobs as she held onto me for dear life. It wasn`t normal for her but I just held her embrace. She had been through a lot with Bobby and now Jafron was gone. I wondered if she would ever find out he was a Fallen.

"They have leads on me," She said in a panicked voice. "They're coming to find me. They're going to arrest me!" she was practically screaming in my ear as she hugged me. She finally let go and ran back inside as I followed slowly. I took my disguise off as soon as I got through the door. It felt good to finally be rid of the fake face that had been taking most of my energy for the past few days.

I looked for Vixen and found her lying face down on the couch her back rising and falling at random intervals as she cried into the pillow in her hands. I went over and placed my hand on her back and tried to speak but my voice had left me at the sight of this helpless girl in front of me.

"I won't let them do anything to you," I spoke softly as I caressed her back," I can't, you're my sister and I will protect you from them. Ok?" She moved slightly and I assumed that it was an effort to say ok. I sat there for the next few minutes with my hand in the middle of her back before I heard a loud knock on our door.

"SOUTH CENTRAL POLICE, LET US IN!" I freaked out and I bent down over Vixen whispering in her ear, "No matter what I was not involved! I didn't know! Ok? I need to make sure I can still help Steve and Roxanne! I will help you, just not right now." She turned and looked at me with her big brown eyes welling up with tears and she motioned for me to leave. I quickly went out the back window and looked back as the police broke down the door and started searching the apartment. I couldn't protect her even though I just said I would.

I heard Vixen scream as the police laid her down on the ground. I knew that I would be able to help her in the long run but right now there was nothing I could do. I just needed to wait until the police had left the house before I could get to the phone. I waited in the back alleyway watching them work through my house.

They finally left later that day at around five in the evening. There was nothing there for them to immediately suspect that I was housing her. It seemed like she was the only person to live there. I crawled through the police tape and tiptoed around the police equipment and little signs that they had used to mark the evidence in the house.

I reached the phone and called Steve remembering his number from when Roxanne had told me it. He picked up the phone after two or three rings and I started to explain to him my predicament. I told him that my sister had committed a crime, the police had come to my house, took her and that they couldn't suspect me. He sat quietly on the other end as he tried to understand exactly what I was saying.

"So you're saying that your sister, Vixen was it? She killed someone and came to you. Stayed with you for two weeks and then as the police were pulling up she told you she had done this crime?" He said with a hint of disbelief in his voice. I knew he wasn't buying my story, but I needed to sell it.

"That's exactly what I am saying. She just told me as the police pulled up so that I wouldn't be suspected of aiding and abetting. I don't even know how they found her here." I started to pace back and forth in my house. I bumped over a sign and a puff of white dust left the floor. I picked up the sign and dusted it off.

"Well, the best thing for you to do would be to go to the police and explain to them that she was staying at your house without you knowing she had done that crime so that they don't suspect you of helping her." I nodded while realizing my stupidity as he continued, "If you're in the house get out now and come and see me. You can stay here if you want."

I thought for a few seconds before agreeing. I quickly packed up my journals in order to keep the Resonance a secret. I had nowhere else to go so I left my house a few minutes later and hopped into my car placing the journals in my trunk. I drove to the police station and did exactly what Steve had told me to and they asked me a few other questions to make sure I wasn't lying like 'When did she come to your house? How long has she stayed there? Did she move around at all?' and a few others. I answered each one in succession and finally was allowed to leave after they took my prints to make sure they didn't suspect me.

I got back in my car and followed the directions Steve had given me to his house even though I had been there a few times already. I pulled up to the crystal white house a few minutes later. It reminded me a lot of Amanda's place but there were a few things that were different. First of all, it was half the size, second it wasn't in the middle of no-where, and third it didn't have the mansion look to it. It did have two pillars on either side of the door as a support for an overhang. It was a quaint two story house with a few windows littering the side.

I shuffled out of my car and up his sidewalk, changing my features to hide my identity again. When I finally reached the door I looked like the same Cornelius that Steve had met back in the diner. I took hold of the gargoyle door knocker and banged it on his door a few times before I heard the shuffle of movement.

As I waited for the door to open I looked around and noticed the perfectly groomed garden. The spotless white shutters. The manicured grass. Everything in its place and not a thing with dirt on it. It was magnificent to look at as compared to the run down houses that lined the rest of the street.

The door swung open and Steve was standing there with a slight grin on his face. He had his gun drawn and I put my hands up as fast as I could. I stood there without moving until he realized who I was. He put his gun down and told me to get inside. As soon as I was inside he put his hand on my back.

"Core, I've been freaking out, after your call I found a note on my table. Nothing was missing, nothing was broken, just a note on the table. It said that I was about to be hurt worse than he hurt Roxanne. Someone is out for us and I don't know why!" As he finished talking he slumped into a chair by the door and put his hands on his forehead. He sighed loudly as I took a seat beside him.

I placed my hand on his back and edged the gun out of his hand as he broke down. I put the gun on his coffee table in front of us. His back continued shaking as I took a look around the house. There were photos of his family littering the walls and everything seemed to be in its place. Most of the items in the house were white with streaks of light blue and gold throughout.

I shifted slightly and Steve started to speak again, "I was worried that someone was out for us when I saw Roxanne's apartment. I thought it was Bobby Thoron's sister but I just found out that she has lived in Montréal the whole time... So, it couldn't have been her. I just don't know what to think right now. I mean it seems like everywhere I go people were watching me. I keep seeing shadows but then they disappear as soon as I look at them." As he was talking I started to piece together what was going on.

Jafron and the Fallen had attacked Roxanne for a purpose and it wasn't to hurt Roxanne. It was to just damage her and make her break down. Destroy everything she had. Now these same people were threatening Steve with the same thing. When Roxanne had first told us the story she had said that the man that had attacked her seemed to be surrounded by darkness. Now Steve was talking about shadows that seemed to be following him. The Skotos were out there and the Fallen were leading them. Jafron had admitted that the Fallen were behind Roxanne's beating but I had to wonder who was controlling them all.

The Fallen knew that all this hardship might hinder their relationship. It was a great plan if it weren't for the fact that Steve and Roxanne already love each other. However, Roxanne was lucky that she didn't have any lasting problems from it. She could have developed paranoia, a psychotic delusion, and a variety of other psychological disorders that would have permanently damaged their relationship.

"I think I know who or what it is but I could be wrong," I told him as I tried moving our conversation to the living room. "I have been looking into love and there are so many reports of love failing that I am starting to think that something unnatural is trying to stop love. Think about what Roxanne described." We made it into the living room as I continued with my hypothesis, "Do you remember me talking about the Fallen and Skotos? They are the embodiment of darkness and they worked against everything God is. Love, Faith, Gentleness, Peace, Kindness, Hope, and more. They may be what is causing all of this. If they are real." I looked at him and he contemplated this idea of the supernatural fighting against him.

"That would be impossible, the supernatural fighting us because we have an actual, real love. Why would they even take an interest in us?" He seemed to toss my idea right out the window and I thought about what that would mean for him. It would mean that the impossible is real. It also meant that he had the pressure of making a relationship work or else. I needed to change the topic quick so that he didn't start actually considering that.

"Well, ok, I can understand why you would say that. It was probably someone who knew Bobby. That's what we have to..." all of a sudden we heard a knock on the door and Steve jumped up and took a hold of his pistol. He used it to open his curtains just a bit before he put the gun back down. He opened the door and Roxanne stepped inside.

"Steve," She called out, "the police couldn't find any sign of another human in my house. They are suspecting that it was all just me. They want to admit me to an insane asylum until they can be sure that I didn't do this to myself!" There wouldn't have been evidence of a human since the Fallen wouldn't leave behind human traces. They were essentially pure corporeal shadows. I knew I would have to fake someone being there.

I took my leave letting Steve and Roxanne discuss the possibility of her being admitted. I took off my corset and hid it in the bushes near his house and then I flew to the forest outside of Kelowna. It was terrifying flying around in broad daylight. I knew that the Skotos bled human blood because of their tendency to eat humans. As they consume the flesh their blood takes on the DNA of the one they eat. The Skotos I had "killed" earlier would have left some blood in the ashen piles. I thought that if I gathered a bit of the blood it might confuse the cops and force them to release Roxy.

I landed just outside of the tree arena. The spherical destruction was invisible from the top but I could see it all as soon as I had touched down. I walked through a gap in the trees and meandered towards the bloodstain. I bent down to touch it and jolted as something grasped onto me. I felt an immense pain that electrocuted my entire body as tendrils wrapped around my hand. A loud burst of laughter corralled from above me. It filled the entire area with the shrill pitches that dipped and rose with ferocity.

"I knew that you would return," An echoing voice sounded out reaching my ears from every direction. The scoffing tone mocking me with every word, "You figured it out. Haha, that we attacked Roxanne and that she would be admitted for wrecking her own house and cutting herself. Heeeehea, she wouldn't have any say because she would be considered insane! Now you're here and I have you trapped. You will not get any my pets' blood." Another burst of laughter bounded in my direction as the light around me began dimming.

"Who are you working for?" I screamed out as I began to gather the light into my body healing it from the constant bombardment of electricity. I used a small, sharp sliver of light to cut the tendrils. I stood triumphantly and started to hover off the ground. The Skotos screeched at me as I had basically escaped his trap.

"I'm shocked you haven't figured it out yet. Heeha. Considering the role he has played in your life from birth." The Skotos appeared in front of me and smiled flashing his blood-stained teeth. He walked around me snickering. "You want his name? Well, if you beat me in a duel I will give it to you. Haheya."

I gathered the light around me and began forming a sword by pressing the light together and making it sharp. The light also formed an armor around me as I flew forward outside of the reach of his trap. Pain racked my body but was being healed by the armor as fast as it was being injured. I raised my sword and faced the Skotos. "Bring it!"

The Skotos bounded at me on all fours with a thorn blade he had picked up off the ground. A shadow surrounding its edge. Our swords collided with the sound of a small explosion, light and darkness meeting in a harsh embrace. I shifted my stance and pushed up on our blades to separate them. He countered and jabbed his sword toward my chest. I took a step to the side as the sword glanced off my armor. The bludgeon took the breath out of me and I had to take a hard breath before swinging my blade upwards to block his next attack.

The Skotos began laughing and jumped back a few feet. He reached down into the ground and began pulling something up from the dirt. He pulled hard and dislodged a large club surrounded with barbed wire. He stepped forward and swung the club hitting me straight in the side of my body and sending me flying outside of the arena. I flapped my wing to try and right myself but hit the ground spewing dirt all around me.

I steadied myself before flying up and diving towards the Skotos. I pulled up just in time to narrowly avoid his club. I touched down and parried a strike from his sword. "This fighting is useless" I cried out as I fashioned a few throwing knives. I flung them at the Skotos and he used his club to deflect them. However, the block gave me enough time to land a direct hit to his chest with my sword. The Skotos crumpled to the ground dropping his weapons which immediately disappeared with a scurry of bugs. I heard the familiar squeal of pain as my sword tugged on the flesh of the beast. Soon after I stuck him into the ground, light returned. The Skotos writhed in pain as it tried desperately to heal itself. The sword was still stuck through his body as he was pinned to the ground. It was trying to shift forms to escape but couldn't. Eventually, it gave up and I used a sliver of light to cut some of the few haggard hairs from his head. I then pricked the beasts neck and let its almost black blood pour into a vial I had fashioned out of light. The rest of the blood sizzled into the ground.

I pulled the sword out of the ground, as the Skotos lay dying, and stabbed it through its skull ending its misery for good. It turned to ashes as the others had and blew away with the wind. I placed the few cut hairs into one of the bags that I had with me. I then heard a flap of wings behind me and I turned to be met with a smiling face.

"My good Jafron, how are you?" I said as he came over to shake my hand. He took my hand and wrapped me in an embrace that I gladly accepted. He seemed to be smiling the entire time.

"I am just great I saw you flying along and thought I would see what you're up to!" He left the embrace and paced over to where he had been bleeding to death only two days before. He paced back and forth over the blood spot on the ground before reaching down and placing his hand on the spot. He then swept the dirt over it so that the forest floor looked normal again. A small sliver of light peeked out his eye as he turned to me.

"Hey, cheer up; you have an opportunity to see the world made better. As long as we can get Steve and Roxanne together. You survived death and darkness, so you should smile and be happy." He smiled again and the tear disappeared as he laughed at the thought him bringing together the couple he had tried to hurt only days earlier.

"Your right," he said, "I am going to help, starting with placing that evidence for you." He then came over and took the bag and vial from my hand before taking off in flight, "I'm in this with you buddy"

As he disappeared into the sun I sat down on the ground. There was something happening inside of me. I felt a darkness in my heart that had been growing since I had the dream where the girl kissed me. I felt like I had been betraying everybody. I wanted to kill the Fallen now and there was a growing resentment in my heart towards the angels. There was a total eclipse happening in my heart. I had felt love without being in love. I had experienced the exuberance of a kiss without actually kissing a girl. I was human in my dream and a Loveless in reality and I had no explanation for my dreams.

I fell to my knees as I bent my head down low to the ground. I prayed there for hours upon end until it was dusk. I took flight and found shelter in an abandoned barn where I began to fall asleep. The last thought before falling into my dreams was, "what if it happens again tonight." Then my mind went black and I fell into the never ending mystery of my dreams. Slowly falling into a realm I didn't understand. A realm of disappearing hopes and confusing dreams.

I woke up in the bed I had become quite familiar with. I left the room and went to the living area where a grand piano now stood. I sat down and started to play. I let my fingers do the work my mind couldn't. A beautiful medley came out that expressed the sadness that I truly felt. In front of me, a blank piece of sheet music started to have notes plastered all over it. The more I played the more notes appeared.

Soon my song came to a beautiful conclusion and right at the top of the sheet a title appeared, "I wish we could be closer". I got up from the piano and started to walk around and see if there were any other differences. It was about an hour before I saw the beautiful girl of my dreams and as soon as she turned the corner my heart jumped out of my chest and fell onto the ground. My mind unprepared for whatever she would throw at me.

Chapter Eleven- Of Deepening Relationships

As she came around the corner the feelings intensified till I was almost hyperventilating. There was no explanation for these feelings, they were innate in my nature, ingrained in the fabric of my being. Then she was finally in front of me, her green eyes shimmering in the sunlight. With the sun streaming through the window there was a golden hue surrounded her form. She had the appearance of an angel, a picture of pure unadulterated beauty. She wore a pair of skinny jeans and a cute red halter-top that accented a near perfect figure. Her hair was now long and curly and seemed to blow ever so slightly like there was a draft in the room teasing it.

She smiled at me before clearing the last few steps between us. I stood there paralyzed by this feeling of bliss that had consumed me. A fire began burning in my heart and spreading to every limb of my body radiating with pure joy. I was now physically shaking under the power of her presence, this feeling blossoming as I felt her nearing me. She placed a hand on my shoulder and looked me straight in the eyes.

I expected to see her eyes changing but they just remained big and beautiful, accented by the slight golden eyeshadow that she wore. She was the definition of paradisiacal in front of me: perfect, immaculate, and from paradise. She was an angel of beauty here to show me what love truly felt like. I felt a tear leave my face and I looked at the ground where the water splashed in an explosion of droplets. It was a human tear, no power remained in it.

She planted a kiss on my cheek before giggling and running away. She expected me to pursue her, so I did. I played this game of love chasing her through the memories hanging on the wall. These ranged from pictures of us as teens to a picture of us getting married. We kept running down this hallway before she veered into a room I had never seen before. I entered into the room and started to look around. There was a bed that was perfectly made and a piano in front of me. Except for those two items, the room was empty. The walls were a dark, deep red which made the bedposts and the piano stand out. I heard her cute giggle from the left of the open door so I entered into the room.

I took one step and collapsed under the weight of my beauty jumping on me in rage. Her fingernails carving out pieces of flesh. I screamed out in pain as I pushed myself up off the ground turning to look at this woman that I loved even though she was a figment of my imagination. Her eyes were bloodshot and her eyebrows were furrowed. Pure hatred flowed from her now where love used to. Her beauty still amazing through the rage.

She moved to attack me again and I backed up onto the bed hearing it creak under me. I was feeling everything as my foot hit the side of the bed. I tried to heal myself but as soon as I tried the lights turned off. I was in her realm, her reality, there was no escaping and there was no healing. Without hesitation, she made her way to the edge of the bed creeping towards me with her eyes fixed directly on mine.

"Why would you do this to me?" She cried, "You're actually breaking up with me? Why would you do that?" She asked each question in the most morose voice I had ever heard. The more she crawled forward, the more I backed up into the wall. The drywall preventing me from moving any further back.

"I didn't break up with you! What are you talking about? I loved what I felt with you! Heck, I love you more than anything else I have ever been presented with. You convinced me to love even though I can't!" I stammered out in fear. She stopped and cocked her head to the left as she continued to stare at me. Her eyes softening as she considered what I said. I could see her thinking, scheming, and planning something.

"You didn't break up with me but you're human. WHY CAN'T YOU BE A LOVELESS?" She screamed at me as she jumped to her feet on the bed. "You've failed me! You WILL fail Steve and Roxanne!" she lunged at me and I rolled off the bed and ran for the door.

"This is your world! You chose for me to be human. I am still a Loveless in the real world! This was your choice" I called out as I ran down the hallway back towards the room I had always woken up in. The hallway started getting longer the more I ran and when I finally reached the door, the angel turned demon had caught up to me.

She reached out and took hold of my arm digging in with her claws that had replaced her fingernails. I felt my skin rip off and I screamed as I stumbled onto my bed. I lay down and closed my eyes tight. I expected to feel her land on me any second but everything was still. There wasn't any sound for a few impossibly long seconds. Then I heard it, a cow lowing in the distance accompanied by the sound of hay rustling along the ground. I opened my eyes and took in my surrounding. The wooden structures informing me that I was back in the real world.

I rolled off the haystack I was lying on and was shocked when I felt a searing pain on my back. I reached around to see what was causing the pain and felt a wet substance. I looked at my hand and saw it covered with blood. I reached back again, feeling for the wounds and realized they were right where my dream had cut me. My mind started to shut down as a thousand questions entered my brain.

What cut me? Did my dream affect reality? Why was she angry? Who was causing these dreams? Could I truly, immensely, and so deeply love a dream? I got up and sauntered outside to a natural spring that was out behind the barn up the mountain a ways. I used the clean water to rinse out my wound. It was still quite dark outside and I couldn't heal. After an initial cleaning, I waded into the water. As I lowered myself I could feel the cold water burning my skin. In the darkness, I could see the water shading over as my blood slowly washed off. It hurt, but it was cleansing.

I stayed in there getting close to hypothermia before I finally decided to get out. As soon I was out of the water I headed back to the barn. My body was numb from the cold and I couldn't feel anything. I sat down and tried to figure out what could have cut me. I went over and sifted through the hay finding nothing. I checked the ground for nails in case I rolled onto one and cut myself. There was nothing though and that confused me. Could dreams really affect reality?

I had been attacked in my dream, that much I knew for sure. My injuries lined up with the attack of the woman. There was nothing that could have caused the damage to me in the real world. So the only explanation would be that my dream caused it. Refusing to believe that, I continued searching the barn for something that could have caused the cuts.

When I couldn't find anything I left the barn and used the light that now blanketed the entire plain before me to try and heal myself. However, the light failed to heal. I found some cloth in the barn and used that to cover up the wound. I still had my powers but they wouldn't work on this problem. I took flight as soon as I could shut out the stabbing pain in my back and began the journey home. I arrived at Steve's place just before five o'clock. I knocked on the door and immediately raised my arms as a precaution. Steve opened the door with his gun fully extended. Lowering it as soon as he recognized me

"Please, come in man." He shifted around to try to see if anyone else was behind me, "They sent us another letter, those people that attacked Roxanne. They are either trying to scare us, or they truly mean it and we should try to get out of here. What do you think we should do?" He said all of this as we walked into the living area. He was sweating pretty badly and I could see that all of this was wearing on him.

"I am sure they are just trying to scare you. Here's the deal, I will look into it. I have resources and I have the mindset to do so. So, you focus on your relationship with Roxanne," As soon as I said that she walked into the room, "and I will deal with these fools. You guys deserve to be happy instead of worrying about this threat." I said all of this with a smile on my face hoping they couldn't see the doubt I had in my heart as I remembered what the dream had just said, "you WILL fail Steve and Roxanne."

A large shattering noise broke the silence that had developed as we thought over what I had said. I dropped to the ground and called out to the others. They chirped back as another pane of glass exploded inwards. When the third one broke we heard the thump of bullets hitting the back wall. Steve took out his gun and started shooting out the window towards the invisible enemy.

The bullets stopped when we heard a scream of pain. One of them was hit. Steve took a hold of the handcuffs he had purchased that were sitting on his coffee table just in case he needed to make a citizen's arrest like this. We all left the house and saw a man lying on the ground with a small red dot growing on his left pant leg.

The man was wearing white pants with a button up shirt. He had snow white hair and I knew he was a Fallen who was pretending to be human. I went behind him, taking the handcuffs from Steve, and cuffed his hands as Roxanne started to ask him questions. As I was behind him I started to try and help this Fallen like I had done with Jafron. Slowly, I saw his wing sockets disappearing off his back. The Fallen slowly crying out as he became human.

After a bit of discussion Steve had him up and in his car with me and Roxanne in pursuit. I was worried about heading into a police station again but as we pulled up I let my fear go. I had to visit Vixen anyways. We entered the building with the Fallen in front of us. The police almost immediately came out to take hold of the limping criminal. One of the officers called for an ambulance to come to the precinct as another began questioning us.

"What happened?" one of the chubbier cops asked us as they led the criminal into the back to await the ambulance. We stood there for a second relieved that the police now had this guy in their possession. Part of our problem behind a glass separation being talked to by a professional.

It was Steve who spoke up first, "My name is Steve and this is Roxanne and Core. We just came from a shooting. We have been getting threats from this guy for over two weeks now. Basically, since him and a few accomplices broke into my girlfriend's house and tore the place apart injuring her in the process. You guys have been trying to solve this case for a while now." Steve said as the policeman took down all of the information as best as he could.

"So he came to your house, shot at it, and you believe that he also came to your girlfriend's house and wrecked the place and assaulted her?" Another policeman who was fairly tall asked as we walked down the corridor to a soundproof room meant to interrogate suspects.

"There was someone shooting at us for sure. It was a fairly fast shooting gun but I didn't see a gun when we went outside. I think he might be just a pawn. Someone else had to have been there as well." Steve said shaking his head. Roxanne put her arm around him to give him some support.

"So you didn't see a gun from where he was standing, is that right?" The cop was trying to come full round. He was using a technique of being roundabout to get the truth out, "And you also shot him once in the leg?"

"What Steve is trying to say is that, in the fray of being shot at, shooting the guy, and arresting him there wasn't enough time to look and see if there was a gun!" I retorted back, now quite angry at the way the police gathered information.

"Alright, no need to get uptight," The cop said as he waved his hands to try and calm me down, "I am just trying to get all of the information!" He stood and paced the room, "Do you recognize the man?" He pointed the question at Roxanne and she just looked at him.

"Yes." She said and both Steve and I looked at her. She then continued, "I didn't recognize his face but his voice was very specific. He was one of the men that attacked me in my room. There were at least two others in the house when they had attacked me." A tear leaked out of her eye as she leaned over onto Steve's shoulder. Allowing Steve to comfort her.

"Alright, we will look into this; there seems to be enough evidence in this story to lock him up after he gets fixed up at the hospital. However, we still have to look at the physical evidence. Your house, the street, and back at the first crime scene, just to make sure you know?" We all nodded and he left the room. We all just sat for the first few minutes waiting for someone to break the tension. When nobody did I spoke up.

"Roxanne, you recognized him?" It was all I could think to say. She looked at me and nodded her head as more tears streamed from her eyes. "Well, when he was groaning in pain and muttering to himself I could specifically remember his voice from that night...At least... At least he's been captured now. I'm happy about that. I don't think we have too much more to worry about. I hope our problems will be done for good."

"What about our houses? Two of them are crime scenes and the third was just shot at so it's going to be a crime scene as well. Where can we stay?" we all just sat mulling over this daunting question. Soon the policeman came back in.

"We have your temporary quarters set up. You'll be staying at the Ramada until there is a house open." A police officer who had just come in said. We all just sat amused that our question had been answered. After another hour of questioning, we all left and headed over to the inn. I was disappointed because I wasn't able to see my sister.

We dropped down onto the beds after a long day of fighting the crap that life had thrown at us. We were all exhausted and fell asleep. My dream was black all night and I wondered why. A Fallen had been taken care of but it was unlikely that that Fallen was the one messing with my dreams once Jafron stopped. So why was my dream black tonight? I wanted some resolve to the narrative of my dreams. I needed to know why my love had become so maniacal.

I woke up more rested than I had been for a while. I went to the bathroom and splashed water on my face. Having a quick flashback to the first dream I had felt anything in. I left the bathroom refreshed and in the form that the couple had gotten to know me in. Roxanne and Steve had just woken up and we all talked for an hour before we left to go our separate ways. I was going to visit my sister, Roxanne was going to get a massage that she really needed, and Steve went to talk to the police about what happened yesterday.

"I'll give you a ride to the station!" Steve said excitedly as I got my trench coat on. We got to the police station ten minutes later and went our separate ways, Steve in through the door to the area that dealt with cases and me through the side door into the temporary jail area.

"I am here to see Vixen Strange," I told the fat cop that had taken the Fallen from us yesterday. The cop nodded and led me to the visitation room to talk with my sister. Soon after that, she ran into the room and to the table that I was sitting at.

"How's it going?" I asked as soon as she was sitting across from me. Her blond hair was messy and she didn't have much makeup on. She looked really rough but she just smiled away.

"It's not too bad in here. I found out that our persuasiveness isn't just when we are a Loveless. I am still quite persuasive." I knew that meant she had good living conditions. She was also a tough girl who wouldn't take any bull from anyone else.

"That's good, anyways," I paused thinking of how I could word it with the police listening, "Steve and Roxanne are so close. They have gone through so much together and their love is so strong right now! I wonder if I should go on to step six, or if I should let it ride for right now."

She looked at me for a while before saying, "Move on, I think right now they need something good in their life!" She smiled at me again before the policeman motioned that her time was up. "I hate that they only give us five minutes. In any case, you can do it just keep fighting!" she said as she got up to leave.

I met up with Steve soon after in the lobby of the police station and he told me that the police had found an Uzi pistol outside of his house and the bullets inside matched that gun. As we got into the car I put the last few pieces of the puzzle together knowing now that only one person had attacked us.

The second man that had attacked Roxanne had to be Jafron. It made sense and it would explain why only one person attacked us. Now one of the Fallen that had attacked Roxanne was actually helping us and the other was locked up in jail. It was also nice knowing many Skotos were also dead and gone. Slowly their numbers were diminishing and it all was because of Steve and Roxanne's relationship. A spiritual battle was being waged all around them and they still were in the dark about that reality. The winning blow was within reach. They just had to get married.

"Do you think you guys are ready to get engaged yet? I think she really needs something happy right now." I said, "She has been shot at, attacked, broken down, and confused for long enough. All the time with you by her side. What do you think?" I turned to see Steve have a blank look on his face. He pulled off to the side of the road and turned to look at me.

"I've thought about it," He paused to swallow and he just sat there for a few seconds, "I've thought about it so much during these last few days but Roxanne and I have only been dating for such a short while. It's too quick. It's way too quick. Right?" He turned around and reached into the backseat. He pulled out a small box and showed it to me. Inside sat a beautiful white gold ring with a small diamond in the centre, "I have it ready when the time is right though!"

As we got back to the inn he hid the ring in the little compartment he had made under the back seat for it and we made our way inside. It was amazing; this feeling of bliss from knowing I had won. I knew that they were ready but the way it would look to everyone would be that they were taking it too fast.

Steve had made the right decision by waiting and I had to get control of all the craziness before I could start to handle a wedding. My sister had told me that the court date for her was set for almost two months later. The wedding would have to be before or after that. I fell asleep feeling content that I had done my job right. Now I just had to keep the storm of anger quiet while waiting for Steve to pop the question.

Chapter Twelve- Of Diving in and Divine Beauty

Days past by slowly after that moment in the vehicle. Every day I expected to hear some amazing news from these people who had very quickly become my family. Each day passed without hearing the news though. Steve was going to propose eventually but he wanted to do it right, both in timing and in stature. Steve had confided in me that if he had half fasted the proposal he felt like it would take away from the amazing relationship that they shared.

So I kept waiting day after day, hour after hour, minute by minute going about my days searching for something to do as I waited for Steve to move into the sixth step. I wasn't going to force him to move forward though because this one had to be his choice. His decision in the end.

The only thing that would break up my days was visiting Vixen in jail and finding out how Roxanne was doing readjusting after the attack. She was strong but I knew that she still hurt inside. Having wounds that would never quite heal and things that would haunt her for the rest of her life. No one goes through the kind of trauma that she had been through and still come out normal.

The monotony seemed endless, not even broken up by the dream that had once haunted me every night. It was gone now, removed from my mind as the Fallen were no longer in control of their power. Peace had finally seemed to settle in and it was calming. I finally felt like things were normal and that maybe, just maybe, nothing else would go wrong.

A week after Steve had shown me the ring I decided to visit the diner. It had been a while since I had enjoyed the simple pleasures of a burger and I knew it was about time to treat myself. I opened the door to the sound of the chime which always brought a smile to my face. I looked around and sighed as the familiar surrounding wrapped me in its embrace. I stood there waiting to be seated for a few seconds when I heard a familiar voice shout from the back.

"Find a seat anywhere that no one else is sitting in. I'll be right out to take your order." Janet called up as she exited the kitchen. She had two plates in her hands and she was looking at them as she spun around the door she had opened. When she finally looked up she started to smile. As I looked at her my mind began reeling. A thought returning to my head. More prominent than ever. I was looking at the woman of my dreams. I pinched myself to make sure I wasn't dreaming but the girl of my dreams was standing in front of me.

Her hair was red and her eyes were the very same beautiful shade of green as my dream girl. She was far more beautiful than the blond haired female I had seen in my dreams. A feeling returned that I had shut out since my dreams had stopped, a feeling of longing, of pure unadulterated desire. I wanted Janet to love me. As this thought crossed my mind a memory chased it down. The memory of that kiss. The memory of the feeling that I could not feel.

The sight of her sent a shiver down my spine and I passed by her. I touched her shoulder and she turned to me and smiled. My heart broke then, I sat down at the soda bar and started crying. The tears were relentless and there was nothing I could do to stop them. I had felt pure love and if it weren't for Roxanne and Steve I would jump at this opportunity. Never before had I been smitten and I didn't know how to process it. I sobbed into my arms for a while drenching my sleeves with tears.

"Are you ok Core?" A soft voice flowed out behind me. "You've been crying here for a while and I don't want you to be sad." Her voice had genuine compassion ebbed into every word. Her heart obviously breaking for this shell of a man crying in front of her. "It's my break right now. Do you want to talk about it?"

I sat there stunned by the thought of Janet seeing me so broken and defeated before her. How could she ever love this wreck of a man and if she did what use would it be anyways? If I loved her back, I would lose my ability to be a Loveless. Without my protection, who would say what would happen to Steve and Roxanne.

Finally, after sitting silently for a while and seeing if Janet would leave I said, "Have you ever loved someone but knew beyond a doubt that it wouldn't ever work between you two?" Every word was crisp and dry, raspy and almost hard to understand.

"Actually, you would be surprised. It happens quite often to me. I haven't found HIM yet. I keep searching but I feel like I won't find HIM even though I keep thinking I do. Each time going through exactly what you are." She spoke each word deliberately, with a sincerity that I had never heard before.

"What if you knew everything in your life would change if you went out with that person. You would no longer be the same. Separated completely from the person you once were. If you were in that situation but you knew the one you loved was close would you still go for that chance?"

"Of course, I would. Love is too important to pass up."

I sat there listening to this woman that I knew I loved and thinking that she was right. If I truly loved Janet what would separate me from that. Nothing separated Steve and Roxanne. Not gunfire, assault, murder, losing a family member, having a father 'go crazy', or even the possibility of insanity. Nothing kept them apart. So why would that be any different for me as Loveless? I asked myself that throughout my meal and every time Janet came by to offer words of compassion or to just to see how I was doing.

I loved Janet and I knew I wanted her to love me too. I finished eating and decided to head back to my house for a nap. I was unusually tired for it being just after noon. However, I had been quite emotional for a long time. So I just decided to give in and sleep. I arrived home just after noon, finally having gained entrance just two days earlier. I walked into the bedroom and curled up on the bed. Ready for more rest.

However, that wasn't the case. As soon as my eyes closed I felt myself wandering into familiar territory. It had been a while since I last experienced the dream. The flowing, changing effervescence of the dream took me by surprise as I meandered once again into the room I knew would be my escape from Janet. I loved her, in my dream at least, and I knew that if I had the chance I would love her in real life too. No matter the cost.

I sat still on the bed waiting for any sign of my dream woman and that is when I heard her haunting voice now immensely familiar singing down the hallway. There was no doubt about it. This dream woman was Janet. This apparition was my diner angel. I got up and headed towards the humming voice. There in the middle of the living area was Janet standing in a wedding dress. I moved closer to her being afraid of what could happen in this dream. With the Fallen dealt with I wondered why I was dreaming about Janet? Each dream had been because of the Fallen. I thought about the possibility of another Fallen being near but waved that thought away as quickly as it came.

Suddenly she stopped humming and looked at me. A melody arising from nothingness and surrounding me. She took a step towards me and began singing,

"I believe in waiting for things you like

Through the fires of hell or the darkest night

In waiting for the power of love to strike

I will wait forever and past the morning light

But forever can end in an instant

And I don't know what to say

I'm afraid that we will lose each other

In the flow of time and space

I hate this feeling

Like it's me who isn't enough

But I know that you're just afraid

To accept I might be your one love

So I will wait forever

Till eternity and back

Till I can hold your hand

And say I've got your back

I will hide my feelings inside the deepest part of my heart

But when you say I'm ready you'll be the biggest part

So let me into your mind and let me be your friend

So that we can be together until the very end."

I sat down on the chair beside her overwhelmed by the simplicity and beauty of the song. As she finished singing she came over and sat on my lap. I couldn't escape it anymore. I was wholeheartedly, undoubtedly, unabashedly in love with Janet. I took Janet's hand and I leaned in for a kiss. She reciprocated with passion and I knew that this is all the dream girl had wanted since I had entered the world. She had wanted me to love her. I was in love and I would soon lose my powers because, when I woke up, I was going to the diner to tell Janet. I couldn't put it off any longer.

Once that decision was made I woke up fully energized. The feeling of Janet's lips on my own still feeling like it was happening. I hoped Janet would love me back, I hoped she would see me for who I was. I got up, changed my face, grabbed my trench coat, and drove to the diner. I arrived there just before the supper rush and I bounded inside. Janet was standing behind the pedestal that said, "Please wait to be seated," and my heart leapt for joy.

I walked up to her and said, "Janet, for months now I have been coming to this diner and seeing you radiating beauty. There is no one I find more beautiful than you. When I came in here earlier I broke down because you reminded me of this girl I fell in love with. One that has been in my dreams for months now but I couldn't figure out who it was. So, when I saw you today. I knew it was you. It had to be you."

She stood there smiling and then opened her mouth to say something. That's when everything stood still. An immense pain shot down my back as I felt my wings being torn from my body. I collapsed onto the floor and writhed in pain. Without warning, two strong arms were wrapped around my own and a blinding light shone in my eyes. I felt myself being lifted off of the ground and being flown somewhere else. A rough wind blew through my hair and I tried to look around and gain some understanding of where I might be. Finally, I felt solid ground underneath of me but I still couldn't see.

The two arms that had flown me to my destination changed their grip and began dragging me up a set of stairs. Each one scraping along the fresh wounds where my wings had once been. After what seemed like an eternity, the stairs turned into a smooth surface and we began our way along that. Finally, we stopped and the arms let go of me. I lay on the ground in pain hoping that the worst of it was over.

My eyes felt like they were on fire but, after blinking like crazy, they were able to make out what was around me. I saw a large wooden pedestal with three chairs sitting in front of me. The chair in the middle much higher than the other two. On each chair sat an angel and above each angel was a nameplate that read, "Loveless, Faithless, and Hopeless." The highest chair was the angel of the Hopeless with the Loveless and Faithless being on either side.

"Welcome, Cornelius Strange." The Hopeless spoke in a sad tone, "We were all hoping you wouldn't have to come here but sadly, even the best fail. You proclaimed your love for a human. Breaking the first and foremost rule of the Loveless. We are so disappointed. Tell us why you did it. What led you to this point? Show us some understanding and teach us what you know so we can understand why you failed. For you are now human and you will be for the rest of time unless you can convince the Elders otherwise. So, the least you can do is give us this account before we send you back.

"So that is everything! All the words I have said before this point. They were my testimony, pure and wholesome, nothing left out. I hope that my word is good enough for them. I don't deserve to be kicked out. I have so many reasons to stay a Loveless, and I have so much work left to do. My testimony is completely open for them. I hope it was good enough."

Chapter Thirteen- Of Debacle and Debate

"So now you know, everything you have heard me say, right up to you calling me here laid out before you. In my opinion, you called me here, pulled me from my life, my work, for no good reason! My testimony is true and I have not told a single lie throughout this account," Cornelius said as he looked around the room before him. The room was gigantic with no visible end in sight in any direction. The white washed view hiding the walls of the room. There was no furniture other than the pedestal that was sprawled out with a few office supplies scattered across it. Behind the pedestal was twelve leather chairs with a variety of creatures sitting on each one. They weren't visible before when he had given his account but as he looked on now he could see them. Each of them wearing a different color robe and each one glaring into Cornelius's soul.

"I don't know if I broke any of the unclear rules that you have set before us but I have laid my case out before you." One of the three angels shifted in his chair before standing up. Large feather wings unfurled from behind him. They grew to their full length and spread across the room revealing their majesty. His chiseled chin and blue eyes standing out against his other rugged features. He had dusty blond hair and was wearing a golden robe. Along the right-hand side of the robe was the name Gabriel written in Cuneiform. He stepped out from behind the desk and made his way over to the seat Cornelius was sitting in.

"We have all heard his testimony," Gabriel began as he placed his hand on Cornelius's shoulder, "this man fought the Fallen and their Skotos, he battled the devil's spawn, kept a couple together, restored a Loveless to his former position, and did all of this while only having access to the

Loveless' power. I have witnessed Steve and Roxanne's love and can attest to its validity." He spoke softly and with conviction, like a lawyer driving his point home. "We must make a decision. However," his tone dropped to uncomfortable growl, "He is not perfect, we all know why he is here. Cornelius Strange, you have been brought before this gathering of Elders because you have fallen in love with a human woman. By the rules of the Loveless, Faithless, and Hopeless you are to have your wings removed, which happens at the moment of failure, and you are to be stripped of your abilities."

Cornelius shifted uncomfortably in his chair as his mind flitted to the woman who had infuriated him since his mission with Steve and Roxanne had begun. That woman who had invaded his dreams, the one whom he loved. Janet appeared on a screen that was previously unseen. The image of her green eyes, red hair, button nose, perfect body figure, and the smile that had pierced his heart on more than one occasion, was in clear view of the elders.

An older Elder spoke up with a crackling voice, "The evidence has been shown to us, both of Cornelius' good, and the clear violation of the law we have set before him. On the screen is what Cornelius is envisioning right now. We know he loves this woman. Tell us, Cornelius, can you deny this love?" The elder motioned for Cornelius to speak but no words came to mind.

Gabriel leaned over to Cornelius and whispered, "it seems like the Elders have already decided but I would still explain your love. Good luck." Gabriel said the last bit with a snarl, his mind made up for itself. He moved aside and began to head back to his chair as the Elders waited for Cornelius' response.

"I do love her. That I cannot deny. Though, she may not love me. So, I would never act on my love in a physical way. Is it a sin to care for someone so much that you cannot think clearly? Is it against your rules to love unconditionally? Yes, but I don't think it should be." He paused for effect, "Hear me out. For you are some of the smartest beings that were ever created." The Elders shook their heads in agreement and one of them said, "Continue."

"The Creator started his work in the beginning with one intention for his creations. For them to love Him and to love each other as well. The connections between Angels and Humans were clearly defined. The relationship between the Humans outlined in perfection but us Resonance were never even mentioned once in the Creator's work. Our rules were put together by you assuming that we were like the angels but we are not. We experience love, we can enjoy relationships with each other. The only thing separating us from the humans are our physical features and abilities. In mind and soul, we are the same!"

Gabriel was nodding as the other elders looked at each other. Cornelius paused as he considered how to end his defense. The silence in the room was thick only broken by the raspy breathing of the older angel. Finally, Cornelius stood up from his chair and walked over to the desk and found a copy of the codex in paper format. He picked it up and returned to his chair but didn't sit down. Instead, he took the paper in both hands and tore it to shreds.

"I think the system needs a bit of an overhaul. I believe the Creator wants us to love! Why would we be imbued with these emotions if we are never to act upon them! I love Janet and I will act upon that love in the knowledge that the Creator planned for it to happen. You have heard of my dreams, each one in succession. The Creator speaks through dreams. He has done this since the beginning and will continue to do so and I believe some of my dreams were from Him. So, when it comes to these rules," he returned to the desk and put the scraps of the rules on the desk before Gabriel. "We will never have freedom. We need to be safe and know that we are risking everything but we should not be forced to give up our gifts. We should get to choose for ourselves if we want to give them up for the one we love! You already have a trial for every rule breaker. Why not pursue punishment on a case by case basis? By the merit of their heart rather than the aspect of the rule broken!"

Gabriel was the first to speak. The entire court time seeming to be led by him, "This is unprecedented, unorthodox, and impractical. However, it is not purely my decision. This is why we have a council of Elders behind us to help make decisions. Let us hear your decisions. Michael, head of the Faithless?" "

"Cornelius," an elder with a blue robe on the other side of the main podium began to speak, "you have displayed faith beyond reason. Your argument makes sense and I believe that love is needed in every sense. I am shocked to hear Gabriel disagree with any decision that leads to practical love! Without Love, what reason would anyone have to believe! Love leads to faith and if someone has a chance to love, unlike us angels, they should take it! Let us rehash the rules a bit. In fact, I vote to place Cornelius on the committee to change the rules."

The room erupted with a buzz of voices as the elders discussed the second vote. Then as the room began to quiet again Gabriel motioned to the third elder who was wearing a lime green robe which was in stark contrast to his white blond hair. "Raphael, head of the Hopeless, what do you say to this?"

"Personally, I agree with Cornelius and Michael." He said from his higher position, "Why would we assume the Resonance to be like us? Let them work with their own rules. We can still guide them in what should be done but let them decide for themselves what should be punished and what should not. Let him love Janet. Let him follow through on the feelings he believes the Creator gave him!"

One by one Gabriel went through the elders and heard their responses. Each of the elders held their own beliefs on the subject and they presented them in full. Ba'ortholemew, head of a faction Cornelius had never heard of called the Warsmiths disagreed wholeheartedly with the entire argument that Cornelius had presented. His blood red cloak flying around with every motion of his hands as he spoke.

Next was Sariph, head of the musicians of the Resonance. They were a group of Resonance without a formal name who worked on songs of worship to the Creator that they would give to humans worldwide. Her robe was a light pink and her black hair flowed down over both of her shoulders covering her name. She chose to let the Resonance make their own decisions.

Then there were three of the trainers for the Resonance. Riely, Flin, and Kroll. All three voted with Gabriel and chose to limit their words to a few choice quotes by famous humans. Each of them nearly matching each other with grey, black and silver robes. Their decisions clearly influenced by the teaching they had done. They taught the Codex as if it were the only law. So it made sense that they wouldn't like someone changing the rules.

The next three were younger looking elders with bright neon color robes. Quin, wearing a neon purple robe, voted against. However, his compatriots, Lyon and Piet, wearing neon yellow and light blue respectively, voted for Cornelius. The three compatriots had been singled out as the leaders of the school system and orphanages for the young Resonance.

Then Gabriel turned to the eleventh elder. "Aleph, head of languages?"

"Personally, I have been impressed with the progress of this boy." He stood up and addressed the other elders, "I am surprised with you all. The Creator loves free will, in fact, he gave the humans choices from the beginning. I know that we were limited from the start but should we limit the ones we don't understand. I agree with Michael, let the Loveless decide for themselves and let Cornelius be one of the new rule writers." He sat with force thinking his point had been clearly stated.

Then a voice that sounded like gravel being pounded on with rocks sounded out, "as with all trials of this kind, the head of that divisions vote does not count. Which means, by the majority, the decision has already been made. Cornelius," The head elder, Jar'el, raised a wrinkled hand that appeared out of his orange robe and pointed it at Cornelius, "You are free to make your own decisions. As for writing the rules for the Loveless. I want you to sit down with Michael and Raphael. Listen to what they have to do in their factions and then create the rules for the Resonance as a whole. After that, you are free to make your own decisions and can chase after Janet if you want. You are also reinstated as a Loveless. To finish your job well."

The room fell into a silence as the verdict had been cast. Cornelius sat there pondering the rules he now had to write. How could he create rules with freedom but also protect the society of the Resonance? He looked up at the twelve elders before him and said, "thank you."

Cornelius stood to leave as his wings flowed out of his back again. Michael and Raphael stood to escort him out. They came beside him and whispered, "Congratulations." They walked behind the lone chair that seemed suspended in midair in the white room. A door fashioned itself in front of him. The frame fusing together as the light faded around the physical object. An oak door stood before them where there was nothing before. They opened it up and a hallway was sprawled out before them. They walked into the hallway and the door disappeared. Michael and Raphael started walking down the corridor passing hundreds of photos that lined the walls. Underneath were names of Resonance that had done great things.

In the first frame, there was a Loveless named Geoff who stood beside Saint Valentine, the patron saint of love. Underneath it said, "Geoff Burthall helped love to prosper beyond what anyone thought possible before." Next to it was a photo of a dead Fallen and a Faithless standing on top of him. It read, "Lynus Aster defeated a battalion of Skotos and Molek the Fallen leader who were trying to trick the council of Nicea into believing a lie."

Down the hallway were dozens of these photos each with their stories. From worshippers who had created famous songs to great warriors who had fought in angelic battles. Each had a small plaque and a large painting that took up the remainder of the room from the plaque, which was just below eye level, to the roof of the hallway. The roof was adorned with a golden crown molding with leaves and flames carved into it. The hallway seemed to just keep going.

All of a sudden Raphael spoke up, his voice had a soft bouncing tone to it, but there was also a force that seemed to come from nowhere on his frail body, "This is a hall only a select few have made it into. Most Resonance never get to see it and the ones who do either end up on the wall or have just lost their...well, you know what happens in there." He trailed off and Michael picked up where he left off,

"Many Loveless, Faithless, Hopeless, Warsmiths, and worshippers wind up on this wall for doing things thought impossible. They changed history, normally for the better. We have people who worked with people like Mother Teresa whose faith was often prodded on by a good friend of hers. One of my better accomplishments."

"Just remember it was your student who did it. not you," reminded Raphael with a hint of chastisement to his voice. "There are people here who went above and beyond their call and often went to every length to do their job to the best of their abilities. Take this man here. His name is Warren Mire-Tyrth." A large Ironclad man was standing holding a shield with the mark of the trinity on it. A medieval marking that was used during the crusades, "The Catholics decided to put together a war after bring prodded on by the Fallen and ultimately by Beelzebub himself. Warren took it upon himself to enlist and try to both protect the ones who truly believed from death and to convince the ones who didn't believe to stop their foolishness."

Raphael looked at the photo with a tear in his eye as he knelt before the photo for a second. Michael chimed in, "he died not long into the war but had already subsided much of the devastation that could have happened. He was a good friend of Raphael's. Each of these people have made some kind of impact on the world and you are the one exception to the norm of those who come through here. You have neither done anything beyond bringing a couple together nor have you lost your wings."

Cornelius reached back and felt the wings that had returned without him even knowing. They continued to walk along looking at the many photos laid out before him. With each came another dart of responsibility. Cornelius knew his job was not over and would be a part of his life forever. Finally, he spoke up, "so, why didn't I lose my wings?"

"You have shown the elders something that is admirable. A desire to follow the will of the Creator..." Replied Michael jubilantly.

"And you have shown a duty to your own faction in a way only a select few have before us. Anyways, we are here." Raphael interrupted as they reached a crimson door that shot off of the hallway. One of the few doors that littered the hallway. They opened the door and were met by the glaring light of the sun. Across from the door was a street bustling with people. As Michael exited the door slammed shut behind them and faded into obscurity as quickly and oddly as it had appeared.

The street didn't seem to mind the three bustling figures. Lining the street were jewel encrusted lampposts each with a pure diamond at the top for spreading the light. The street itself seemed to be made of perfectly cut Golden blocks arranged into a pattern with the cracks forming crosses the entire length of the road. The sun seemed amazingly brilliant but as Cornelius searched the sky he couldn't find a singular light source. In fact, beyond that oddity, he also couldn't find a single shadow anywhere around him.

Every building was perfectly outlined and clearly visible but there wasn't a single shadow in sight. No darkness at all in the general facility. Across the street seemed to be a few buildings each with names that couldn't be read. They were in an odd writing that was incomprehensible to Cornelius. The buildings were all perfectly formed with many colorful aspects to them. One building with a longer name had red wooden shutters that were surrounded by a spectacular shade of Yellow making up the rim of the window. The building was made up of slats of redwood that had been stained a beautiful yellow-white. The door was a light blue.

"Follow me," said Raphael as he made his way towards a much larger building just to the right of the shop. On the outside were three symbols that were completely unrecognizable to Cornelius. The first was an arrow surrounded by what looked like a heart, the second was a book with a sword down the middle being used as a bookmark, and the third was a fig leaf suspended in the middle of a feather that crossed perpendicularly with it.

Raphael motioned to the building and said, "We are going to speak in here. This is the head office for the Resonance factions. Love, Faith, and Hope as symbolized by the markings. For the Loveless a heart and an arrow describing the swiftness and sharpness of love. For the Faithless a book and sword to describe the Sword of the Spirit and the Word of God which all true faith is based on! Then there is my faction, the hopeless with a fig and feather to remind us of the dove which returned with a fig to Noah after years of being on a boat within the turbulent waters.

The outside was the same color scheme as the other buildings along this path. They entered into the office passing large marble pillars that seemed to have been carved directly out of a cliff. Each one with depictions of angelic battles carved into them in spectacular detail.

After making their way past the entranceway, that reminded Cornelius of the Loveless stronghold, they made their way down a few floors till they reached a room with a large parchment and a table set out with three chairs. All of a sudden Michael spoke up and said, "Well, I guess the elders beat us here and set up for us." He sat down in one of the chairs and motioned for Cornelius to follow suit.

"Alright, Cornelius." Raphael began, "First we need you to understand our missions before you can write these rules. You need to be able to cover all the factions in these rules and they should be precise and able to be used for court. It sounds intimidating probably because that is exactly what it is. The last set of rules were prepared by the elders before the Babylonian exile of the Jews."

"It's been a while," Michael picked up, "each of the factions, as you know, protect one of the three main actions of faith that will remain at the end of time as set forth by the creator. You are well versed in love, being a Loveless. It is the most important of the three and is responsible for both faith and hope. Believe it or not, it has actually been in existence since the beginning of the Resonance. They just ran in secret until the society became too big."

"Love for the Creator is the greatest commandment," Cornelius said nodding his confirmation to everything the elders had been saying. Cornelius quickly surveyed the room they were in. It seemed to be a theatre of sorts with a large stage and curtain at one end of the room. There was writing on the wall to the right of the table that was written in an unknown language. Cornelius tried to understand what the words were for a few seconds before continuing to scan the area. The room was far too large to be an office space so Cornelius assumed that they put it together just for him.

"Exactly," chimed in Raphael, "and as such it must continue to be important in the world. With Steve and Roxanne, they just might possibly have a chance of starting true love again. As for our ministries, we are slightly different. For the Loveless, you have to watch over two humans and turn them towards each other. It takes effort but it isn't impossible. Some of what the Faithless and Hopeless do is. Michael, why don't you explain what is going on in your faction and explain the basics of what a Faithless does."

Michael shifted in his chair and leaned forward clasping his hands together, "the Faithless exist to keep faith in the world. We battle against 4.2 Billion People who disagree with Christianity and try to help the 2.8 Billion who say they believe in continuing believing. Which is not easy. Every day there are new scientific studies that try to prove evolution true. Every week, a new hate group comes out who tries to blaspheme the name of the creator. However, every year there are hundreds of millions who are hearing the gospel being preached and a large percentage of those who hear are coming to believe. We regulate that, help with the process, protect Christianity against the work of the First Fallen, the Fallen themselves, and the Skotos. Currently, evolution is the biggest topic that we are battling against."

"That sounds like a lot of responsibility," exclaimed Cornelius, "how do you do that?"

"A large workforce is helpful, but we fail a lot. We accomplish our task by sending out Resonance into areas of contention against Christianity or areas of great conversion. Iran is one of the biggest battlefields right now."

"Wow, that is... Well, it's spectacular. What rules do the Faithless have to follow?"

"The main rules like never falling in Love with a human. Also never purposefully showing yourself to the people you are working with, meaning they have to keep disguised while on a mission. Those are the main ones. The minor ones included things like remaining close to the Creator personally, keeping powers hidden from evil sources, and never doing anything to prove or disprove Christianity."

Cornelius sat there thinking about the mission he had been given finally realizing just how hard it was going to be. He had to make a succinct ruleset that covered three enormously diverse factions and make it so that the rules would be able to be used for years to come.

"Right now," Michael continued, "we are dealing with a war that is brewing. It is based on a temperamental element in the Earth that could be the key to discovering what created the universe. The Faithless that have been working on this have had their hands full with minor firefights happening on a daily basis. No group has sole possession of this element which means no one has had the time to study it. Well, that is what we tell everyone but in all reality, we don't know where the element is. It has disappeared and the original worksite is impossible now. In my opinion, I think that the best thing would be to destroy the element but we can't do that. So, that is the fun I have to deal with. Raphael, why don't you tell him about the Hopeless?"

Raphael smiled and said, "This will be fun. There are three main aspects to the hopeless. First, we try to keep the general public from becoming too distraught. Second, we try to work with the faithless to keep Christianity alive and well and thirdly, we work with evangelists around the world who preach the word of God. Overall, the Hopeless can be summed up by saying that we work with humans to give them hope. Obviously, the greatest hope any human can have is the word of the Creator but we often need to go into broken and desolate countries and show them a new way. People like John G. Paton and Hudson Taylor were accompanied by Hopeless in some form or another."

After he stopped speaking he looked around and nodded at Michael. Cornelius had started to think and he had sat down at the desk that was provided for him. He picked up a pen and said, "Thank you, I hope that I do this right." With that Raphael and Michael left the room. The silence was calming and Cornelius smiled as he looked at the pages. He bowed his head and quickly prayed, "Creator, you know what needs to be written. You know us best. I need you to help me now!"

Cornelius sat for a while figuring out just what he was going to write. Each one had to be all encompassing. All of them had to be able to be followed but still strict enough to rule the factions. The first rule had to be "Love the Creator with everything you are." The second closely followed, "Love each person you come across in a way that you can help them in the true heart of your faction, be it love, faith, or hope." And finally the third rule would be, "Use any means to help your target, so long as it does not go outside of the bounds of the word of the Creator."

The rules were general but they fulfilled each of the faction's expectations. Cornelius sat for a day in this new place writing out smaller rules for each of the factions. Rules that governed love that would be proper for a human and Resonance, others that spoke to how to properly reveal yourself to a target, and still others that governed the basic interaction between the different factions. The new rules opened up the world of the Resonance to each other. If a Loveless wanted to be a Faithless they could. If a Resonance wanted to be human, they could.

As Cornelius was writing the door opened and Gabriel entered in. "How is it going?" He came over and looked over the rules that were written. A majority of the rules were written down and others were scribbled on papers to get the wording right. Gabriel looked for a while before saying that everything looked good.

Cornelius finished writing them not long after Gabriel left the room. Each rule dealt with the heart of the ministry that the Resonance took part in. He took the manuscript and began walking towards the door he had come in through. Without warning, it opened into the same courtroom he had been in earlier. Another Resonance was sitting in a chair being judged for some crime he had committed. His black hair and dark complexion stark against the white background.

Gabriel was on a tirade when he looked over and saw Cornelius. He stopped midsentence and motioned for Raphael to come and get me. Within seconds, Raphael had taken me back into the other room.

"So, I guess this means you're finished then?" He asked as we walked over to the table I had been using for so many hours. He grabbed the rules and unfurled them. Looking at each one and then looking straight up as if considering the meaning of them. After a while, he turned and congratulated Cornelius before touching him on his head and he blacked out for a second.

* * *

When I woke up Janet was smiling and staring at me, "Are you ok?" she giggled, "you professed your love and then passed out. I was kind of worried about that." Her voice was slightly sarcastic but it still had a tone of compassion to it. I shook my head trying to get rid of the haziness that had quickly consumed me. I looked up and thought I was in the dream. Trying to make heads or tails of the vision that I had seen. It seemed like it had all happened from a distance. Like it hadn't actually happened. The pain was excruciating as my body caught up with the day and a half that I had been in court. The whole time fitting into a few minutes of real life. I stood up and reached behind me. I felt the familiar ridge of my wings and breathed a sigh of relief. It wasn't a vision. I had actually rewritten the rules of the Resonance.

I stood up and smiled at Janet, "It is terrifying to tell someone that you love them. Especially someone as beautiful as you." Immediately she smiled and turned her face to hide her blush. I grabbed her hand and asked, "What do you think of us trying out a relationship. There is no one in the world that I would like to get to know more than you."

She smiled and said, "I get off in an hour if you would like to take me out on a date." I agreed and began heading out to set up the best date I could. I got reservations to a small mom and pop restaurant on the outskirts of the city near a small mountain path. I went and bought a bunch of lanterns from a store nearby and began setting them up along the path creating a romantic atmosphere all the way to a small lake that had a mountain rising behind it. There was no wind that evening and the lake was perfectly still mirroring the whole scene.

After setting up the lake I headed to my house to get a suit. I put it on before going and buying a beautiful dress for her. I arrived five minutes before she got off and waited outside the diner for her to be finished. She came out of the diner with a huge smile on her face and I got out of the vehicle in my suit holding the dress for her.

"Is that for me?" She asked with a very excited tone of happiness. I handed it over and she headed inside to get changed. She came out just beaming in her gold dress. She got into the vehicle after I opened the door for her.

I started the engine and said, "There is no one I would rather spend this evening with than you. I have been dreaming of this moment for so long. Literally." We began the trip towards the restaurant as we discussed what my dreams meant and how long Janet had harboured feelings for me. The more we talked the deeper the passion I felt in my heart. A burning feeling that grew to an inferno throughout the meal. Every joke she told, every time she mentioned her faith, and every time she told me about her life I fell more in love with her. She was perfect.

After the meal, we headed down the path. Her eyes lit up by the lanterns. Her hair glimmering as we walked down the path. She kept spinning as she sung out songs about love. Her joyful nature just permeating the forest as we walked. Soon the path opened up to the lake with the moon perfectly glimmering off the surface. We walked to the edge of the lake and s*at down facing each other.

"This night was so awesome. More than perfect." She sighed as she lay back on the sand. I took the hint and lay down beside her looking at the stars. She reached over and grabbed my hand, "I hope that you stay with me. I really, truly like you."

"Of course, I will, as long as possible." We sat under the stars for what felt like hours talking about everything under the sun. After a while, we got up and walked back to the car. I went to open her door and when she came close she leaned in and kissed me. Immediately all of the heavenly bodies aligned and exploded in a rush of power. In that moment, I knew she was the one for me. Forever more, I would love her.

Chapter Fourteen- Of Dates and Devotion

It had been two months since Steve first showed me the ring and a lot of things had happened, the police finally caught a suspect for the Gersch break-in, as they were calling it. Also, Steve and Roxanne had gone on many dates mostly because of my money, or "generosity", of course, all I had to do was persuade some people to let them in for free. They saw it like I was helping them anyway. Also, my relationship grew immensely with Janet. Every day falling more in love with each other.

It had been quick but everything just seemed to fall into place. Soon after Janet and I began dating Roxanne was able to move back into her place and after all that time I too was also allowed back into my home. It had been a long time but my home was still the same as before everything right where I left it. The only thing that had changed were the relationships around me. Now Steve and Roxanne had gone from good friends to talking about marriage in only a month and then after two they were planning their lives together.

So much had happened in the short year that I had known the couple. Within the last three months, without trying, they had become a symbol of love. Everywhere they went people would stare at them and long for what they had. Sometimes coming up to them and asking for advice on how to be happy. All because they had a feeling that couldn't be explained. It was a mixture of happiness and fear for failing, of passion and power, and of forever and eternity.

In this short period of time between wanting to get engaged and marriage, there were many things that could throw a wrench into the relationship. They could get angry and decide that they didn't like each other, they could bring up long gone issues and try to rehash them, or they could continue on without any problems. I wasn't worried because they truly loved each other and were willing to work through any issue.

I had left the house early in the morning and saw Steve sitting in his car looking at me. I went over and he rolled down his window, "Hey Steve, how are you today?" He looked at me with a huge grin on his face and he just motioned for me to get in. I got into the vehicle with a sigh and saw the box sitting in the cup holder in the open for the first time since he had first shown me. I looked over at him and he turned to me with a mixture of emotions on his face that I had never seen on him before. It was a look of elation, fear, and passion.

"We are going to C'est L'amour tonight. I've thought for so long about marrying Roxanne. Tonight I want to go through with it. We are going to the place we had our first date and I would like you to be there, in the booth beside us!" Steve said with a huge grin on his face.

"I'll meet you there. You go and get Roxanne! I'm so happy for you guys and on such a beautiful day too!" I hugged him then left the vehicle to drive over to C'est L'amour. I entered in and found out where Steve was going to be seated and hid in the booth beside theirs. It was only a few minutes before I heard Steve's noticeable laugh. I had done this so many times before it almost felt natural to be listening in. Steve sat down and I closed my eyes to listen to what they were saying shedding a tear for this beautiful relationship that was becoming finalized.

Steve started right away as soon as they sat down, "Roxanne, over the course of these last few months I have fallen deeply in love with you." I heard some rustling and I peeked around the corner to see Steve taking hold of Roxanne's hand. It wasn't odd for Steve to be saying sweet words to her. He almost constantly was either complementing her or telling her that he loved her.

Roxanne spoke up when Steve paused, "I have fallen for you too Steve, we both know that. I love you, so why would you say that?" She said almost as if she knew about the engagement. She said it in a cheerful tone and almost mockingly. I heard Steve chuckle after she finished talking.

"Well, I just wanted to let you know. Thanks to Cornelius we practically reintroduced ourselves, grew together, and became much more than just friends. Most of that happening to some extent here. I mean, I feel like this," He motioned to him holding her hand, "was there before but he gave us the means to try dating. I would have been too scared otherwise, you know because you are just too beautiful and amazing. I was scared but now I know what I want in my life, and it's you." He lowered his voice as he was talking and started to speak in a very sincere tone.

"Awe, Steve that's why I love you. You always know what to say. I've needed to go on a date with you, a real date, for so long now. I'm so happy you took us here." Roxanne had started to speak in that same low and sincere voice that Steve was talking in. It was like they were connecting through their voices and not just their words. Words can mean anything but tone says a whole lot.

"Well I was hoping you were going to be happy, that's what I want for us from now on," I heard rustling and I saw Steve move around to the edge of the table he took a glass and used a knife to make it ring out a few times before he spoke in a loud voice, "May I have your attention. This lady here is the most beautiful girl in the world and over these last few years, she has been the best friend, and now girlfriend, a man could hope for."

There were a few deep breaths and then he continued, "I want for her to be happy for the rest of her life and I don't want any other man to be there for her like I will be." Steve was beaming as he spoke in a loud voice to let everyone know what was happening. He then took Roxanne by the hand and knelt down on one knee. He pulled out a small wooden box hand engraved with a heart on the top of the box, "Just like this box is hand-made so is our love and I want that love we built together to last forever. I love you and I don't ever want to lose you. No one could make me happier than you do so I ask you today," I heard him take another deep breath, "Will you marry me?"

Roxanne almost screamed with delight as she said yes. She jumped up from her seat and gave Steve one of the most beautiful kisses I had ever seen. Then everyone around the restaurant clapped at the beauty that they had just seen. Finally, I felt relaxed knowing that all my hard work had paid off.

Then Steve looked over at me with a tear of happiness falling off his cheek, "what a coincidence," He laughed, "Cornelius is here!" He seemed genuinely surprised. Though I knew it was an act. It seemed like he wanted her to believe I was there on my own power and not him inviting me. I got up and made my way over to the couple hugging each one in succession.

"Congratulations guys and just so you know I have done wedding planning before if you want someone for free!" I thought I would mention that because I had put together multiple weddings before. This one would be my honour to put together. I was so happy!

They finished their dinner together and then invited me over to their house to celebrate their extremely recent engagement. As we began heading out my phone rang and I picked it up.

"Hello?"

"Hi, this is the South Central Police Department, is this Cornelius Strange?"

"Yes, what seems to be the problem?"

"Your sister has been missing from the jail for almost a day now and we have begun a search for her. Has she tried to make contact with you?" His voice was stern and somber. I couldn't believe that she would try to escape. That wasn't like her.

"Sorry officer, but I haven't seen her since I last visited the precinct almost a month ago." My mind was moving at a thousand thoughts a second to see if I could figure why she would try and escape, "If I do see her I will call you right away."

The officer sighed and said, "Alright. We'll keep in touch if we find any developments." With that, he hung up the phone and I shook my head. Roxanne asked me what was up and I told her that Vixen had escaped from jail. She had a worried look but I told her to not worry. It was a happy occasion and she didn't need to think about my problems. I got into my vehicle and pulled out the wine coolers that I had picked up at the local liquor store. I pulled up to Roxanne's house and saw Steve and Roxanne getting out of their car.

We went into her house and were shocked when we were met with a blast of frigid air. A look of fear overcame Steve and Roxanne's faces. There, standing in front of them, was a Fallen in his natural form, challenging me in front of Steve and Roxanne. I couldn't fight him in front of them and I couldn't just let him get away with revealing himself so I started thinking about how I was going to deal with him.

"Steve, Roxanne, run I'll take care of it. Just trust me. Run!" I screamed at them. Steve took the lead in trying to escape but as soon as they began to turn a bolt of ice shot across the floor engulfing the couple. The Fallen had frozen them in their tracks. The ice rotating their bodies so that they were forced to watch me take on this spawn of Satan. The ice slowly took to life and started to cover them from the neck down in a thick sheet of ice. Their heads still uncovered so that they could breathe and see but their bodies were frozen so that they couldn't move. There was nothing I could do either. I had a choice to make, I had to act now and show my true form or fight this demon without using my powers. Neither seemed like a good option.

I couldn't help but look back and see the pain stricken faces of Steve and Roxanne as their body parts were slowly freezing. I had to act quickly or else they wouldn't survive. I started to reach over to take hold of an umbrella that was beside me. When I felt the cloth in my hand I quickly picked it up and hurled it towards the demon who leaned slightly to the left so that the umbrella stuck into the wall behind him. The force driving it far enough in to make it hang on the wall. I took the few seconds he was distracted to move into the living room where I saw a vase with a carnation in it.

I had to keep moving or else I might lose one of them to hypothermia, or frostbite. It was a challenge but I could do it. I smashed the vase and heard Roxanne gasp when she heard the glass shatter. She was still so afraid of those people breaking in again. Those people that I now knew were Skotos and Fallen having fun with us. Those people that were standing in front of us tempting me to show Steve and Roxanne that I was a Loveless.

I took a piece of the shattered glass and slowly flowed some of the light into the sharp edges. It was now powerful enough to hurt the demon and I would still seem like a human that just seemed really brave. As I took aim with the glass shard the demon jumped forward hoping to get at least one hit in. His hideous fangs protruding from his mouth like a saber tooth tiger hungry for his next meal. His pure red eyes searching mine for fear but I showed him none. I just slashed at him as soon as he was within range. The Fallen stumbled back and I knew I had struck him. He screamed in rage as I prepared for another assault.

"Tell me you name. I need to know your name!" I told the Fallen knowing quite well he wouldn't answer me. "You shouldn't have come here. Now I'm going to make sure you never leave."

With that, the demon screeched and jumped towards me as I held up the shard. The demon landed squarely on the glass and gave out a shout. He began disintegrating as the light struck his heart. I couldn't help but wonder if he would be the last of them. I knew they would never give up, but considering the circumstances I sure wanted it to be over.

I went over to the couple and touched the ice. The moment my hand touched the ice it shattered and disintegrated just like the demon. It was dark inside of the house and once Roxanne and Steve were free I went to turn on the light. I flicked the switch but it did nothing. The power was off or perhaps there was another Fallen in the house.

"You guys stay here I am going to make sure there aren't any others!" I told them as they hugged each other to get warm. What a way to come into an engagement, being attacked by creatures of darkness. I made my way through the house slowly checking each room for one of the beasts I was certain I would find.

Finally, I came to the room that I had found Roxanne in only a few months ago. Standing on the bed right over the place where Roxanne had been weeping was a Fallen. His pure black wings were darker than the blackest night, standing out against the darkness of the room. His eyes were redder than the deepest blood red. His stature was regal and he snarled at me when he realized I was there.

In this position, he seemed almost majestic being outlined by the void that shrouded this dark monger. He stood there staring into my eyes with a ferocity that resembled an angry lion protecting his cubs. There was something behind him but I couldn't see what was there.

"Why are you here? You know you've failed. They are engaged and soon they will be married. You can't fight that. You can't even fight me." I explained to the motionless body I saw in front of me. I waited for a response and when all was silent I moved. I took the light infused glass bottle and went forward to attack the beast in front of me. Still he just stood there motionless, dead to me and the circumstances of his situation.

As I moved forward cautiously I noticed something odd about the room. A flicker here and there as if mirrors were set up around the room. I started to pull my shirt off to let my wings fly free. The entire time being guided by the illumination from the glass which created a small aura right in front of me as I continued to walk.

I needed to see what was around me. I needed to find out what those glimmers of light were. I thought about my sister's escape and shed a tear that splashed on the ground. A short second later lighting up the whole room. The faces of ten or more Skotos were lit up with the light of my tear and I realized my mistake.

At once they pounced, shrieking with an unearthly ferocity. I knelt down and covered myself with my wings. When the first few Skotos hit me I fanned out my wings sending them flying into the walls. However, that didn't stop them or even stun them. Within seconds, I had a handful of them covering me.

I was overwhelmed as claw and tooth hit my skin. I felt the sting of them striking my body with rapid fashion. I swung relentlessly with my glass and hit one of the Skotos directly in his head causing him to burst into ash. This caused the others to pick up their speed. It didn't take long until I was feeling weak and helpless. The light from my tear wasn't enough to heal me. I was dying from the injuries I was getting from these demons. There was nothing I could do and I was losing hope.

Without warning, the weight of the Skotos on my back ripped away allowing me to attempt to stand. I tried to keep attacking slightly skimming one here and another there but never taking them out. There were too many of them and I was too weak. I was outnumbered and out powered. I looked up and saw the Fallen laughing uncontrollably above me.

I shed another tear which hit a Skotos that I had gotten right underneath of me which made him squeal in pain. I stuck him as he struggled to get the watery light off his head. He evaporated as they all did and I was able to get onto my feet.

Even though I was up there wasn't anything I could do. I couldn't cry and I couldn't hit them so I just started to give up lowering my arms to accept the next attack. Right then I heard a shuffle from the door to the room. I heard one of the Skotos who had latched onto my back grunt and three of the other demons left to go see who was at the door. Each one squealed in pain soon after they had left. They had gotten hurt by whomever or whatever was at the door.

I reached around with the glass and cut off another demon whose fingers were still embedded in my back. I threw the glass at another one of the demons who got it right through the head. It fell and shattered into a thousand pieces. The pain in my back was intense as the claws that still poked out of my back moved as I did. I used up some of the light from the second tear and healed a few of the cuts that were on my back as I turned to see who was there.

I turned to the door to see the silhouette of a Loveless and two humans. I knew that Roxanne and Steve were the humans. They both held crude knives that seemed to shine as if they had light flowing through them. The Loveless had a light sword in his hand that was speckled with the ash of a Skotos that he had just taken out.

Steve and Roxanne were both angry as they rushed into the room to aid me. I fashioned a sword from the light of my tear and hit one of the creatures that was charging at me. The sword went right through his stomach as he continued running making him flake off and spray all over the room covering most of the room in a faint dust. The darkness started to fade as the last Skotos was dispatched. The Fallen stopped laughing and disappeared in a puff of smoke as I thrust my sword towards him. As the smoke cleared I could make out the object that was behind him that my sword had sunk into. I immediately let go of my weapons as I recognized the object in front of me as my sister. It was her human form with a crude form of wings sewn onto her back. The sword slowly dissipated leaving a hole in Vixen's body.

I started to break down as I saw my sister dead in front of me. I clenched my fists and hit the ground as I screamed out to try to get rid of the pain I was feeling. Roxanne moved up beside me and placed her hand on my back. My scream quieted and I winced as her hand touched one of the cuts. She moved and gently pulled out the Skotos' claws. The pain was intense but partially relieving. I was crying tears that took away the rest of the darkness in the room and I couldn't help it.

My sister was dead, the people I was helping knew I wasn't what I seemed, and I was in pain from the many wounds I had on my back. I couldn't stop the flow of tears that came out of my eyes. I realized that I was crying more than I had ever cried before. The room was soon blinding with the light that radiated from the puddle of tears I had formed.

Through the brightness, I saw a note on Vixen's body and I went to take it from her. As I pulled the note from her hand her body shifted so that she took up the feeble position I had found Roxanne in. The demons had set it up so well to the very detail that it brought on a second wave of tears.

I unfolded the note and stared at it for a few seconds. The room was quiet as no one wanted to speak first. I read over the note a few times before I looked up at the stunned faces of Steve and Roxanne, as well as the other figure hiding in the background.

"What does it say?" Steve said, finally breaking the silence as he moved into the room. He sat down on the bed as I tried to compose myself.

"It says, 'If you are reading this you survived my trap and your secret is now discovered. It is only right, as you took a Fallen from me, that I take away your powers by having you come out in full fashion in front of those you are trying to help," I paused a second to look up at Steve and Roxanne who just nodded at me to continue, "It then goes on to say some things about the Codex which is our rulebook. Then it says, 'This attack was meant to kill you but if it didn't then the pain of losing your sister, your clientele finding out, and your losing your powers will do the job for me. The Fallen will not be beaten. Never. Try as you may. We will survive. Look for me or don't. You will not find me. I don't want to attack you again but don't test me. Start looking for me and you will be stopped by my army. Signed, The First Fallen"

We were silent as we let the words of the letter sink in. The being who I thought was a Loveless, who had been in the doorway, stepped into the light of my tears and I recognized him right away. His regal face and proper stature told me that he was an Angel but it was his stunning lime green eyes that gave away who it was. Gabriel had come down to help me. Somehow he knew about the attack, either that or he was following me. In either case, he had saved me. He had also witnessed me revealing my true nature to Steve and Roxanne. The new rules were less strict but they still banned showing the humans the true nature of a Resonance.

"Don't worry my son. This trap was meant to show you to the people you care about most. According to those rules you wrote this is pretty bad, but I can let it go because of what has happened between this couple tonight. In fact, I feel like Steve and Roxanne needed to know. So you don't have to worry." He moved over and placed his hand on me as the light in the house returned to normal. I used the light to heal the few wounds I had left as Steve and Roxanne moved beside me.

"So what are you? An angel? And what were those things?" Steve said as he sat down. He looked confused, not believing what he had seen on the day he had asked Roxanne to marry him. This day was filled with so many emotions that no one could understand. There was happiness, anger from being betrayed, sadness from being attacked again and having Vixen die, fears from seeing a demon, confusion from seeing me in my true form, and most of all disbelief of everything.

"My name is Cornelius. I really do want to help you. I love you guys as friends but I am not human. I am a Loveless. Not so much an angel, but not fully human either. We are like the Cupids from Greek mythology. A creature called a Resonance. We are the keepers of love, faith, and hope. The ones that are fighting to keep love alive," I paused for a second to let that sink in, "Those things you saw were the Skotos I had told you about before and the tall guy and his cold friend were Fallen. They are basically demons sent to stop us from accomplishing our cause. They want us to stop because if love exists they cannot rule the world which is what they want. They showed themselves to you because you are engaged and meant to be in love. They knew they had to act and they knew I would try to protect you."

For a few seconds, the air was thick with the words I had just said. Both Steve and Roxanne were breathing shallowly. They were overloaded with information that was impossible to comprehend. It was as if I had just explained infinity to them, they were unable to understand the complexities of it.

"So you're saying that we were the last hope for love and because we are together now," Roxanne said as she looked at Steve lovingly, "we can keep true love alive? So are you able to keep helping us then?"

I looked at Gabe and he nodded. I then hugged Roxanne and Steve, "Yes I can. I want to see you guys get married. Now there shouldn't be anything to stand in our way. I don't think the First Fallen will interfere again but if he does we will have some Faithless to protect us. Gabriel, could you get Michael to send some to protect us?" Gabriel nodded and I got up and started to pace at the thought of the leader of the Fallen attacking us again. His real name was unused in the Loveless society but he was more commonly known as Beelzebub, Lucifer, or Satan whichever name you wanted the feeling of fear was there. I continue to pace as Steve and Roxanne sat.

Finally, Steve spoke up, "we want you to be our wedding planner. I know you hid the fact that you aren't one of us but that shouldn't hinder the fact that you brought me and Roxanne together. I think she will agree with me when I say we want you to plan out the wedding and I personally want you to be my best man!" He came over and placed a hand on my shoulder as I stopped pacing, the pain of my dream wound still affecting me. I slowly went over to sit down.

"I completely agree with Steve; I want you to be with us through every step of planning this marriage. You brought us together, you brought us closer and now I want you to be there when we are married!" She wrapped her arm around me as Steve sat back down. Gabriel stood in the corner smiling from ear to ear.

"You see Gabe, the codex was wrong about one thing," I said as I raised my voice like an announcer for a football game, "In certain situations meeting the people you are bringing together in your true form is good!" With that, Gabriel laughed, turned, and left the room with only a bang of a door closing to tell us he was gone.

"So then it is settled," I wrapped my arms around them in an embrace, "I'm planning your marriage. I still have to hide in the form you normally see me in, mind you." We left the room in order to get away from Vixen's body. We then sat in the living for the next few minutes tossing around ideas about table settings and who they were going to invite. I was happy that they accepted me as someone helping them. I was happy they were finally together and I knew that there wasn't much else that could go wrong. I would protect them at all costs.

Chapter Fifteen- Of Defining and Deciding

It had been a hectic month since the final attack at Roxanne's place. We avoided her house like a plague fearing what could be inside. Roxanne had put it up for sale not long after the attack and began staying in Steve's basement. We had become a close-knit family as we planned every detail of the wedding. They had accepted me as the crazy uncle that could help with anything they struggled with.

There were times where I could see that true love breaking through and within those moments I always felt a longing to be with Janet. After Steve and Roxanne got married I would get married to Janet. She would be my love for the rest of time. Her face had haunted my dreams for years and now she invaded my mind almost all the time. It was perfect though, another beautiful image of love.

Sleeping was no longer a problem since the Fallen were taken out. My dreams were once again beautiful interpretations of my subconscious and everything seemed better than ever. I was still caught off guard by that one single solitary phrase in the note. "The First Fallen." The king of the Skotos and the Fallen, he had told me to stop but I wouldn't. I would give my lives for this couple to be together. I didn't understand why it was so important for me to fail. I knew keeping love alive was important but for the king of demons to put his forces against me because of it, it was too much to understand.

That fact loomed over us as we continued with preparations. Each day we would begin by figuring out how we would contact each other if a Fallen attacked. But apart from that planning, we also had a wedding to put together. We already had flowers picked out, the church set up, and most of the people invited. In a month, we had done so much for the wedding but what truly mattered was how well Steve and Roxanne worked together. If Roxanne wanted something, Steve would get it for her and vice-versa. They were perfect together. The wedding was now only two weeks away.

There was so much to do in that little time. I got up early to go and see Roxanne about getting the cake. I drove over to the house at around ten in the morning stopping to pick up a coffee for her. I pulled up and Roxanne was just locking the door to Steve's house.

"Hey Core," She said as she left the house and came down to get into my car. When she was inside she said, "I want to go do some dress shopping today if that's ok and I want you to be there. We need to get that now. I can't believe I put it off for so long."

"Why do you want me to be there?" I asked as we were driving to the cake shop. We were heading to la patisserie, a French cake bakery on the Southside of the city. They were well known for their three-tier, red velvet cake. I believed that was what Roxanne wanted. The cake wasn't important though, as the dress needed to be bought now.

"I want you to be there because you are my best friend at the moment and you seem to have good taste in clothing from what I have seen you wear." We talked for the drive to the shop and arrived there around lunch. We went in and were met by the fantastic aroma of cookies and cake baking. One of the chefs came out to the sound of the bell ringing as we entered. He came up to meet us and shook our hands before we told him that we were there to get a wedding cake. He invited us into his office to get our order.

"Welcome, bonjour. How can I help you today?" The man said with a hearty laugh as he flopped down onto his lazy boy chair. He seemed certain anything we threw at him he could handle.

We went through all the details and then dropped the bomb on him. "The wedding is in two weeks. Do you think you can have it done by then?" Everything in the last month had flown by and all that was left was the dress and the cake. Everything else was taken care of and after today so would the cake and the dress.

The cake master nodded his head and told us it would be close to two thousand dollars for the cake. We agreed and sauntered out of the store leaving behind a very hectic baker behind getting his crew ready for the order they had just received.

I got into the car with a sigh as I realized my journey with this couple would soon be over. All the time studying their history, fighting the demons trying to keep them together, all of it was coming to an end and it disappointed me. I had grown close to the couple in ways I couldn't explain. That feeling from my dream came back and I realized that in some sense of the word I loved this couple. I loved the fact they were together, that I helped, and that they were getting married in two weeks. It was all so overwhelming that I felt myself getting dizzy, these new feelings taking over.

We drove for a while before getting to the dress boutique. It was a simple store with dresses lining the windows but when you stepped inside your eyes were overwhelmed by a smorgasbord of beautiful gowns of all shapes and sizes. There were marble pillars on either side of the entrance draped with silk ribbons and flowers. In front of us was a small desk with a thin lady with her hair in a bun.

"Hello there, how can we help you today?" the lady asked with a vivacious tone to her voice. We sauntered up to the counter taking in the pictures of beautiful ladies in immense dresses with beautiful bouquets in their hands. They all seemed to have a regal stature to them as if they were judging our humanity and our imperfections.

"We need to find the perfect dress today for a wedding two weeks from now!" With the challenge set before her, she led us into the actual shop with dresses being fit out by perfect mannequins. Dress after dress passed by until we entered into the back room.

When we entered the back room our eyes lit up like we were entering into Narnia. It was amazing the rows of dresses that seemed to stretch into the infinite spaces of the white walls. It was a breathtaking sight. The lady leading us brought us right to a specific dress as if she knew exactly what would suit Roxanne.

The dress was a black sequin mermaid fit dress with white accents throughout. It was a strapless dress with a six-inch train behind it. The dress was beautiful and Roxanne immediately went to try it on. She came out a bit later wearing the dress and it was a perfect fit. She turned to the lady with a huge smile on her face and sweetly asked, "Do you have this dress in white with black accents?"

The lady nodded in agreement and took her to the directly opposite side of the dress room and pulled out the exact same dress in white. "Sorry, I should have shown you the white one first," She apologized before handing the dress over to Roxy. She tried it on and when she came out of the dressing room time stopped. The light seemed to be swallowed by the dress bringing attention to her radiant face. Her beauty just shone through and she had tears in her eyes.

"This is the dress and it fits perfectly. Can I buy this now?" Roxanne asked with tears in her eyes. The lady led her to the counter with her still in the dress and put arrangements together for the cost. It was apparently a two-thousand-dollar dress but the lady gave her a discount and gave it to her for fifteen hundred.

After a short period of her changing out her dress, we left the shop laughing and talking about the month that had gone by since Steve had popped the question. It was just about five by the time we got out of the shop and we called Steve for him to meet us at McDonalds for food.

"I can't believe it was so easy for us to get the dress and the cake," She said sighing as we drove to the nearest fast food restaurant, "I just can't wait till all this stress is over and it is just me and him against the world!"

I took a while to think out what I was going to say next because it was going to be hard for me to say, "You do realize I'm not going to be able to stay here once you're married, right?" We pulled into the parking lot and as soon as we were stopped she looked at me.

"Why not Core, you don't have to leave." She paused for a long time before she continued choked up, "what if Steve and I need help, and what about Janet?" As soon as she said her name my heart leapt with joy.

I couldn't help but smile politely and say, "Well, I'm hoping Janet will come with me and we'll be married soon after you guys. I am hoping to get engaged soon after your wedding. There will be another job though so I must move on." She looked at me with a glimmer in her eye as she mulled the thoughts over in her mind trying to find some way for me to stay.

"What if we need you? What if the Fallen return? How will we spread the love? You need to stay here with us. We need you Core." She pleaded with me as each question came out. I couldn't help but feel that tug to stay. My heart had truly grown fond of these amazing people. I loved having them in my life and I hoped that it could continue in some way.

"To be honest Roxy. Once you're married you will have Steve and he will have you. You'll be able to look out for each other. The Fallen might return but I'm certain they will follow me once I leave here. As for spreading love, just show people how you two love each other. Being willing to show affection in public, love freely, forgive easily, and people will keep asking you why your love looks so different than theirs."

"I just wish you could stay." As she said this Steve came up to the window and knocked startling Roxanne. He beckoned us to come into a coffee shop that was across the street from the restaurant.

We went in and talked about all the money being spent, the time we put into everything and we just felt a great sense of accomplishment. Finally, in two weeks all of our hard work would pay off. Soon hundreds of people would come to enjoy their final connection to each other. It was intense, amazing, and was all over done.

Over the next two weeks, I made final preparations for the wedding like setting up the chapel and the reception hall for the two hundred guests that would be coming, all the time remembering the girl of my dreams and the love that we shared. Not long after Steve and Roxanne got married Janet and I would also take that step. We would be together in love.

Soon it would be all over. There were only a few hours left until their big day. I didn't realize it that morning but it was already the last day I would be a part of their lives. The last day I would not give myself completely to love. The last day Roxanne and Steve would be apart. It was the day of the marriage and there wasn't much left to do. I had so many people checking and double checking everything I knew that the wedding would go well.

I woke up early in the morning and I found out that Steve was waiting for me downstairs. He was a nervous wreck and I could tell that there was something on his mind so I sat him down on my couch and we started talking. "So man, are you nervous or are you just shaking because you're cold," I asked with a concerned look on my face. He looked at me with tears in his eyes as I watched him tremor.

"I... I am just so afraid that she will have second thoughts about me!" He spoke slowly as if considering each word, "God has given me so much and I have thrown it away but I want so badly to keep this one. I guess I am still a little self-conscious." He laughed and smiled at me.

"God will give her to you I know that much!" I told him as I placed my hand on his shoulder, "Look at this girl you have. She is the perfect match for you and she knows you are the perfect match for her. She would be crazy to have second thoughts. Do you mind if I pray for you?" He turned and looked at me with a look so pitiful I couldn't stand it and we both bowed our heads in reverence. "Oh Creator, I pray to you today to ask you to watch over this day. I know your plan was to bring Steve and Roxanne together. Continue to do so in everyday life. In their everyday ministry. In your name only I pray that you do your will in their lives. Amen"

At that moment, the door opened and the limo driver told us it was time to go. Ten in the morning and we were already heading out for a two pm wedding. We entered the limo and started our drive out to the chapel that was selected for them. We pulled up to the old fashioned church with its cobblestone pathways and tall steeples.

The scene was beautiful with flowers littering the ground outside the door and a beautiful white archway marking the entrance to the chapel. We stepped in and were quickly escorted to the second floor of the building where we were placed in a small room to wait till the wedding started.

"Man, do you think that we were meant to be?" Steve asked nonchalantly without a care.

"Of course, man, like I said the Creator had a plan for you and right from the beginning she was part of it!" I said as I sat down on the wooden chair that was placed beside an oak desk. There sitting on the desk was a tuxedo meant for me. I put it on quickly as we waited for the call to say the wedding was starting but we knew that we had to pass the time somehow so I went out to find something to do.

As I was walking I heard the girls talking and I decided to pop in and see the bride. I walked in and was met with a huge hug, "Can you believe it's today already! I can't and it's my wedding!" Roxanne practically yelled in my ear.

"No, I can't believe it either! It's insane! Steve is just a ball of nerves. He really loves you Roxanne and you're lucky to have..." I paused as I noticed the green eyes staring at me from a distance. The Red hair was what caught my attention. I saw Janet and fell away into daydreaming thinking about how much I loved her.

"Have what Core?" Roxanne said trying to get my attention. Finally, she snapped her fingers and I came back to reality, "What was that about?"

"You're lucky to have Steve!" I said before walking over to Janet and embracing her while giving her a kiss. She came out of it dazed but smiling, "And I am lucky to have you, Janet, more than anything in my life, I am happy to have you."

I got down on my knee and pulled out the ring that I had stored in my pocket that I just couldn't hold onto any longer. I looked at Roxanne quickly before turning my attention totally to Janet and said, "Janet, please marry me. I can't live without you." She jumped for joy and said "YES!" I placed the ring on her finger and then left to go and check on Steve, after making sure she was ok with celebrating later. After sharing the news with him we had to wait for another two hours.

As the time drew near Steve turned to me smiling, "I am so ready for this now! I can't believe after all this time of my liking her I am finally going to have her to myself!" He sat smiling and we decided to talk to fill in the last few minutes. We talked about a lot of things including Janet. We couldn't stop talking about how we were perfect because we had seen Roxanne and Steve from the beginning and we could both have a good relationship because we knew what to do.

Finally, the time came and we heard a knock on the door. We opened the door and a man ushered us out into the hall and downstairs to our respective spots. Immediately, as I was standing to the right of the groom I noticed those green eyes staring at me. We both smiled and watched as the doors to the chapel opened and the light blasted through around the silhouette of Roxanne. Never had anything looked so truly angelic.

She walked down the aisle slowly taking her time to let Steve breathe in the beauty he was seeing. As I looked around I noticed a few familiar faces. Jafron, Amanda, and even some of the other Loveless were there to witness the final step of the last chance for love coming to fruition.

She finally got up to the pulpit and I heard her whisper to Steve, "I love you!"

The ceremony went on and the preacher talked about true love taking the message from 1 Corinthians 13, "Love what a beautiful thing. Mistaken, broken and confused in today's society but when true love brings together two people like Steve and Roxanne we can know that it still exists and that we still have a chance for true love. Love is never a mistake for it is willing to wait, and is always friendly. It isn't a mistake because it doesn't envy, and people who have it aren't stuck up. They also don't put others down or insist on getting all the credit. Love doesn't lose its temper in bad situations or hold grudges. Love hates evil and looks out for others before itself. Love keeps trusting God and will always expect the best. The thing most people hate about love is that it is forever and never ending. But you are here because you want to make that commitment." The preacher said with a strong, beautiful voice.

Soon everybody in the audience watched as they exchanged rings and Steve recited his vows, "Roxanne, I love you and throughout the few months we have grown together I have shown you true love. I stuck through your problems and have waited for years for you. I have been your friend through thick and thin and have never questioned your decisions but my love isn't shown through that. My love is shown because I am willing to be with you forever, no matter what."

Then Roxanne spoke with tears in her eyes and her voice shaking from the tears, "Steve, I love you and there is no doubt in that…" She took a second to regain herself then she continued, "Through thick and thin, through bad times and the good, through everything you have been there for me and me for you. I hope that we can be together and I promise to make that wish come true."

Then the priest said, "I am pleased to announce you Mr. and Mrs. De'Lemit. You may now kiss the bride!" Steve kissed her and they went out of that place and kept that promise they made for 80 years. Never wavering in their love for a second. Everyone who saw them would ask them about love and in one year there were hundreds of new and blossoming couples being watched out for by the Loveless. Through their example, a world was changed. Soon others had the same idea to settle down and true love started to blossom once more.

Of Epilogues and emanations

Two months later we all got together for coffee at the diner. It had changed ownership since Janet and I had left the city. So we sat down and talked about everything we could think of. We talked about the semi-celebrity status that Steve and Roxanne had quickly gained with people daily asking them why their relationship was different. In the background a television spewed out a small news story with the title, "Element is missing in the Egyptian war. Tension building."

Steve looked at us and smiled before speaking up, "So, Core, when's the big day?"

"We're getting married in three months today. In the same chapel you guys were married in. Core has been fairly busy with his work in psychology. Bringing more people together just like he did with you two!" Janet said.

"Yeah, I moved two cities over to one of the larger conglomerates of my company." I said as I winked at Steve, "My current client is dealing with the recent loss of his mother and he is slipping into depression."

We all chatted for a few hours about life, work, and after a while, we finally decided to go home. As I got up to leave a man in the corner of the cafe stood up and called me over to him. I walked over to him and saw the trench coat he was wearing and knew he was hiding something.

I reached his table cautiously and he stood up with the coat barely moving so that it still concealed his face. He looked at me through the darkness that hid his face, except the piercing red eyes, and spoke just ten words, "you've won this one but this is not the end."

This is the first book written by Chris Luchies. This was a passion project written as the beginning to a trilogy. The second book, Faithless, is already being written and is hopefully going to be completed near the end of the year 2017 or early 2018. The third book, Hopeless, will follow a few years after that.

This book was written with many Bible verses in mind but must be understood as a piece of fiction. This book is not meant to be theological in any way. There are some theological truths in this book but there is also a lot of things that do not exist. I hope you enjoyed the antics of Cornelius and the Loveless.

Christopher Luchies

"And now these three remain: faith, hope, and love. But the greatest of these is love." -The Apostle Paul (1Corinthians 13:13)